UndeR
THE
WiLLOWS

A NOVEL

PAMELA McCORD

FROM THE TINY ACORN . . .
GROWS THE MIGHTY OAK

Under the Willows
First Edition

This story is a work of fiction. References to real people, events, establishments, organizations, or locales are intended only to provide a sense of authenticity and are used fictitiously. All other characters, and all incidents and dialogue are drawn from the author's imagination and are not to be construed as real.

Book cover by Ebook Launch.

Book interior design and formatting by Debra Cranfield Kennedy.

www.acornpublishingllc.com

ISBN—Hardcover 978-1-947392-94-6
ISBN—Paperback 978-1-947392-93-9

UNDER
THE
WILLOWS

PROLOGUE

It began with a conversation with my son.

"Dot was crying last night," TJ said through a yawn.

"Dot? Who's Dot?"

"You know. Dot. Alexa's Dot."

I stared at the back of his head, frowning, as I dished up his breakfast.

"Alexa can't cry. It's a cylindrical inanimate object. Are you sure you didn't imagine it?"

"Mom. I'm eight. It really did happen." He looked at me with a scowl. "I don't imagine things."

And he didn't. But that comes later.

First, here's where it started.

CHAPTER 1

Tom's death changed everything.

I sat in my car, the engine idling, staring at the cheery yellow Victorian. I wasn't cheered.

We'd been planning the move before Tom . . . went away, but now I was making it alone. Well, with our son, TJ. Tom had inherited the yellow house from his grandmother when she passed away several months ago. He'd flown out to look it over and reported back that it needed some updating but had good bones. He said there were lots of rooms, which sounded like heaven in comparison to our tiny two-bedroom in the city. "It has a *huge* country kitchen," he said with a grin, slipping his arm around my waist. At the time I was chopping veggies in the postage stamp that passed for our current kitchen. I leaned my head back against his shoulder and sighed, daydreaming of endless countertops and cupboards in our future home, giddy at the thought of all the space.

I had a right to be bitter. A goddamn drunk driver snuffed out my husband's life. All that crap about forgiving. I would not forgive the one who stole him from us.

Everyone was quick to say that holding on to the hate I feel for Mr. George Goddamn Daniels would only poison me and not bring Tom back. I felt the poison in me now, but embraced the huge empty hole eaten away by the acid-generating hatred. I didn't want to feel good, because everything's bad.

In the rearview mirror, TJ's 8-year-old face was sad, like mine. He gazed at the yellow house, not moving to open the car door. Maybe the two of us could stare it into becoming our home.

"Ready, buddy?" I asked as I opened my door. My heart broke at his wan smile and "Sure, Mom."

Tom had seen the house, but I hadn't. I had no idea what awaited us other than lots of rooms. I fished the key out of my jeans pocket. It had resided in that pocket all the way from New York. I guess I thought it might help me to bond with our new life or something.

It wasn't a gingerbready house. Not spindly and frail looking. Not tall and narrow. It was sprawling, with a wide wraparound porch and stone steps leading up to the front door.

Catching sight of TJ as he surveyed the exterior, I swallowed tears that threatened to spill out as I thought how different everything would have been if Tom hadn't died. My little boy would be jumping around in excitement, grinning and waving his arms, impatient to get inside. He would have burst through the door and run from room to room. Tom and I would have taken our time as he ushered me into the foyer and kissed me a welcome home. I felt the ghost of a smile trying to find its way onto my face as I pictured the three of us—

Stop it! I brushed angrily at my cheeks. I needed to turn this house into a home for TJ and me. Tom would have wanted that.

No eight-year-old should have to lose his father.

My son's eyes were flat as he watched from the safety of the sidewalk as I fiddled with the old key in the old lock. He looked away as if he didn't care whether the door opened or not, his shoulders hunched, his head down. He kicked at a pebble, his hands shoved deep in his pockets.

"Come here, buddy," I said, sitting down on the top porch step and holding out my arms. He shuffled up the walk and sat next to me. I draped one arm around his thin shoulders and hugged him to me. "We're gonna be okay. I know it doesn't seem like it now, but you and I are going to make this our home and be happy here. It's okay to be sad. I'm really sad, too." I lifted his head and looked into his eyes. "You and me . . . we're gonna take care of each other."

I sighed and hugged him, his little blond head tucked under my chin. "You can talk to me anytime you're feeling sad, or if you want to talk about Daddy. I hope you'll let me talk to you when I'm feeling sad, too. We need each other now." I ruffled his hair. "Okay, buddy?"

I stood and brushed off the back of my jeans. "Let's go check out our new home."

He hung back when I pushed open the front door. The inside was dim, the late afternoon sunlight not strong enough to pierce the heavy drapes covering the windows. A musty smell from the house being closed up assaulted me, and I covered my nose for a moment to give myself time to adjust to the odor.

I looked around through air inhabited by dust motes. "Wait here," I told TJ, as I carefully opened the drapes at the tall front windows. Even with the windows uncovered, it wasn't bright inside. The overhang from the large wrap-around porch blocked direct sunlight from shining in. Still, it was bright enough, considering the state of our mood.

"Wanna look around?"

TJ shrugged listlessly. The feeling was mutual.

"Let's go pick out your room." I tried to infuse my voice with as much enthusiasm as I could muster, but it sounded hollow, even to me.

"Why did we have to come here?" His eyes showed his hurt and anger. "All my friends are in the city. I won't know anybody here."

I sighed. "Because this is what Daddy wanted for us."

His face scrunched up, bright tears shining in his eyes. He glared at me. "Daddy's not here anymore."

"You're right," I snapped. "He's not, and he won't ever be again." Ashamed, I turned away so he wouldn't see the tears that filled my eyes, too. I gulped a breath, struggling for control of my emotions. "I'm sorry, buddy. I'm having trouble dealing with losing Daddy, just like you are. I didn't mean to snap at you."

He stared at his feet, not meeting my eyes.

"There are a lot of reasons we came here. Adult reasons that you shouldn't have to care about. Just know that I love you and I'll do everything in my power to give you the best life I can."

I bumped his shoulder with mine. "Come on, buddy. Forgive me?"

He put his arms around me, resting his head on my chest. "I'm sorry, Mom."

I held him out and tilted his face up to look at me. "We need to get out of this mood we're in. I'm tired of being sad. Aren't you?"

"Yeah, but what can we do?"

"For starters, let's go pick out your room." I pasted on a smile and turned him toward the stairs.

CHAPTER 2

In the two weeks after we arrived in Marysville, we'd settled in pretty well. TJ had chosen the bedroom at the opposite end of the hall from mine. It looked out over a forested backyard, complete with a tire swing in the big old oak closest to the house.

I set up a Dot, the small, compact Alexa unit, in his bedroom, like I had in his bedroom in New York. TJ often asked Alexa to tell him a bedtime story, and his father had recorded himself reading *Treasure Island* for Alexa to play for TJ. I hoped it would make his new room feel more like home.

I let him pick out Spiderman bedding to make his room more appealing and told him he could paint the walls blue and red if he wanted. Anything to bring a smile back to his face.

And joy. What I wouldn't give to see joy in my little boy's eyes. Maybe the same could be said about me, though.

The furniture Tom's grandmother, Kate, left him was in pretty good shape for its age, and most of it wasn't even smotheringly old-persony. Bad me. We got it for free. Who was I to judge her taste? It was a blessing really, since most of our furniture back in New York had been the rental variety that came with our apartment, and I'd managed to donate or sell odds and ends we'd no longer need in our new home. All we brought with us was our personal property. And memories of Tom.

Actually, the home was charming and comfy in a lived-in kind of way. Kate had taken good care of her possessions, and there was no need for me to replace anything immediately. I picked out some colorful throw pillows for the oatmeal-colored couch and put away her crocheted doilies and arm covers. A lot of crocheting had gone on in this house.

I'd only met Grandma Kate twice, first at our wedding and again when TJ was a year old. He was her first great-grandchild and she was excited to meet him. She was elderly already and didn't like to travel outside her little town. I think that may have been the last time she did. We were busy with our jobs and our son, always intending to visit someday but never quite getting around to it, so I never got the chance to know her well. From her home, however, I could deduce some things about her. She was organized and tidy. She loved antiques and knickknacks. There were shelves of porcelain cows. She loved cows, especially the black and white Holstein ones by what I gathered from her collection.

A loud knock startled me out of my reverie. I opened the door to see a man in a postal uniform.

"I wanted to introduce myself. I'm your mail carrier," he said with a tip of his hat. He tried to unobtrusively peer around me to see inside the house. When I crossed my arms over my chest, he cleared his throat and stepped back. He held out his hand. "I'm John Brindleson."

"Pleased to meet you, Mr. Brindleson," I responded, taking his hand. "I'm Kelly Harris. My husband Tom was Kate's grandson."

He nodded. "Kate was an institution around here. Everyone loved her." He shuffled his feet. "Is your husband with you?"

Although he seemed personable, I didn't know John Brindleson from Adam and wasn't eager to share that I would be living here alone with my son. "Not at present," I answered. I didn't plan to keep secret the fact that Tom had been killed, but now wasn't the time to get into the weeds about his death, especially not with a total stranger.

"Oh," he said. "When will he—"

"Mr. Brindleson, I don't want to be rude, but I still have a lot to do around here. It was nice to meet you, but I've got to get back to it."

"Oh, okay," he responded. He seemed disappointed that I didn't want to set a spell, so to speak.

I smiled politely and closed the door as he stepped off the porch.

Brindleson was a large man. Even though he looked to be in his fifties, he was solid and, I have to say, intimidating. I'm sure he was a perfectly nice person, but I still didn't want to advertise that I was a single mother living alone.

Back in the kitchen, I popped a coffee packet into the Keurig well. Sitting at the white-painted gate-leg table, I spread out the *Marysville Times*, a small local paper which was delivered daily to my front porch. It was getting close to lunchtime, and I wanted to relax a few minutes before calling TJ down for lunch.

I noticed an ad for a youth camp for kids 7–12 provided by the Marysville Methodist Church. I perked up at the thought it could help TJ make friends in town, and called the number in the ad to sign him up to start Monday. The camp ran daily through the summer, from 9 a.m. to 4:30 p.m., with outdoor activities like hiking and swimming. TJ would like that, whether he knew it or not. And I liked the fact that his being in camp all day would give me an opportunity to more fully explore Marysville.

CHAPTER 3

TJ didn't jump at the idea of going to summer camp. I wasn't surprised at his reluctance, as no part of this new life was easy for him. He wanted to dig in his heels to prevent me from thinking he was okay with my forcing him to leave his familiar life behind and move to this unfamiliar place. Prepared for his pushback, I reminded him of our vacation in the Berkshires one summer when the three of us hiked to a lake and Tom showed TJ how to fish. TJ had talked about that trip for weeks afterward.

"Daddy won't be there," he responded.

"I know, sweetie, but you'll still have fun. And maybe you can make some new friends."

I held up my hand to ward off his upcoming *but I already have friends* by saying, "You're not going to replace your old friends, but wouldn't it be nice to have friends here to play with? When school starts, you'll already know them."

He shrugged, but didn't complain further and, come Monday, he was ready for me to drop him off at the church.

I introduced myself to the pastor and the camp counselors and inquired about Sunday services, as I thought my argument about making new friends should apply to me as well. With a parting, "Have fun," I drove away, trusting God to watch over the most precious thing in my life.

My first stop was the Bank of Ohio branch on Main Street to transfer our accounts from our New York bank. No, my account. My meager account which wasn't so meager anymore. The life insurance that Tom had insisted on maintaining after TJ was born had paid off. A cool two hundred and fifty thousand dollars. It would make life easier for us for sure. Not that it brought me any pleasure to have such a healthy balance, but I couldn't deny that it would come in handy until I found a job. I hadn't worked since college and, even then, my only job had been waitressing. That wasn't a bad thing, but it was hard work and long hours, and it would take me away from my son. Because of Tom's career with a tech company in New York, I'd been able to be a stay-at-home mom, which we both agreed was best for TJ. For now, I wasn't going to rush into anything. Not until I was sure we were on an even keel in our new town.

I stood uncertainly in the bank lobby until an attractive young woman approached and introduced herself as Jennifer Brennan.

"How can I help you?" she asked after leading me to her cubicle and offering me a seat.

"I need to transfer my bank accounts. I just moved here from New York."

"Oh, well, welcome. I'm sorry. I didn't get your name."

"Sorry. Kelly Harris." I rummaged in my bag for my latest bank statement. "I'm not sure what the process is. What do I need to do?"

"Well, let's get an account set up for you. Checking or savings?"

"One of each."

"We can open each with a minimum balance until your funds are transferred. Can you do $500 for checking and $50 for savings? If not, I can see if we can lower the initial deposit amount."

"I think that will be okay. I'll write you a check for cash and you can use that. I don't need to go back to New York to close that account do I?"

"No, you should be able to take care of that online, or by phone. You'll just need to provide them with your new account numbers."

"Great. It will be good to have that checked off my list. There's a lot to do when you move."

"Tell me about it," she said while typing my information into the computer. "What brings you to Marysville?"

"My husband inherited an estate from his grandmother, Kate."

"Kate Harris?"

"Yes. Did you know her?"

"I did. It's a pretty small community, in case you haven't noticed. She and my grandmother were life-long friends. I spent a lot of time at Mrs. Harris's house."

"What a nice surprise. Maybe I could contact you if I have any questions?"

"Of course," she replied, typing my information into the computer. "So, you and your husband moved from New York? Do you have any kids?"

"I have a son. And my husband isn't with us. He passed away the end of November."

Jennifer's eyes widened and reflected a moment of concern. "I'm really sorry. It must be doubly hard on you to be in a new town so soon after losing your husband."

"You have no idea. It's . . . it's . . . been tough. And tough on TJ. He's my son."

"Look, I know this is presumptuous of me, but would you like to grab some lunch after we're done here? I can tell you about the town and you probably don't know many people here yet—"

I felt an immediate sense of gratitude. "I would love to. The only person I've met so far is the postman, Mr. Brindleson."

"Probably not someone you'd picture as best friend material."

"No kidding." I laughed. "He seemed like a nice man, maybe a little nosey."

Half an hour later I followed Jennifer out of the bank.

She looked both ways down Main Street. "Let's see, I'm not sure what you like. There's Molly's Pie House, kind of an everyday café-type restaurant. Really great cherry pie and burgers. Or we have Italian, Mexican, some chain restaurants—"

"I'm not picky, really. How about Molly's Pie House? Can we walk there?"

"We could, but it's the end of June and pretty hot. I don't want to be all sweaty when I go back to work. I can drive."

The inside of the diner was all mid-western cliché, with its black and white tiled linoleum floors and red vinyl-covered booths. It was early for the lunch crowd, so we got a table right away. The menu was pretty middle-America comfort food, just as cliché as the decor.

"I didn't ask if you're a healthy eater, being from New York where I'm sure everyone is into fitness, and you look like you're in great shape. Maybe you won't find anything you like here?"

"I'm a 'when-it's-convenient' healthy eater. Definitely not vegetarian or vegan. I'm craving a burger so this is perfect. Being new in town, I don't want to become known as that typical uppity New Yorker who turns her nose up at comfort food."

"That sums me up, too. By the way, my friends call me Jen. You can, too, if you want."

"I appreciate it, Jen. You're my first friend in Marysville." I contemplated the fact that I'd just met her and she immediately invited me to lunch, and that I pegged her as a friend so quickly. Maybe it's a small-town thing.

"You haven't met any interesting people since you moved here?"

"Not really," I said, taking a sip of my water. "I've mostly been getting used to the new house. Putting things away, arranging cupboards and drawers the way I want them. I did a little exploring around the town, but mostly I've been sticking close to home to help my son settle in. I'm only out and about today because I enrolled him in the summer camp program the Methodist church offers."

"Oh, yeah. I've heard it's popular with the elementary crowd."

"I hope so. TJ needs to find friends. It was hard on him leaving everything he knows in New York, especially his friends. I think he was angry with me for dragging him out here."

"I bet. The church camp should be a good place to make friends." Jen had shoved her sunglasses onto her head when they'd come in out of the sunlight, and now she took them off and tucked them into her purse. "What does TJ stand for?"

"Tom, Jr., after his father. We used to call him Tommy, but he thinks that makes him sound like a baby. We compromised on TJ."

Jen glanced up at the approach of our server.

"No more talking," I said. "I have to devote myself to this burger!"

She laughed around the bite she'd just taken, nodding in agreement.

CHAPTER 4

I had a friend. I was surprised how relieved I felt at the thought. Suddenly, I wasn't facing my new future alone. I sniffed. One lunch doesn't a lifelong friendship make. She might not even like me after she got to know me. And *vice versa*. But, still . . .

I pulled up at the church at four fifteen, not wanting to take the chance of being late and causing TJ to worry. Turns out, I had zero reasons to be concerned. He got off the bus with two other boys, the three of them looking thick as thieves. His beaming face caused me to smile and let out the breath I hadn't realized I'd been holding. When he spotted me, he waved, then said goodbye to the other boys, and raced to the car, his face full of light. Happy.

"How was it?" I asked as he climbed into the car.

"It was totally cool," he said, his little-boy face animated. "We hiked to a waterfall."

"That *is* cool. And it looks like you made a couple of friends?"

"Yeah."

"Yeah, what? Do they have names?"

"Oh, Mom. Of course they have names." He grinned at me, teasing.

I poked him in the ribs. "Give, big guy!"

He settled back in his seat, reaching for his seatbelt and pulling it across his chest to click into the slot. "Mike and Kevin."

"Mike and Kevin, huh? Are they good friend material?"

"Yeah, they're cool. They'll be here tomorrow. I'm coming back tomorrow, aren't I?"

"Sure, if you want to."

"I do." He started fiddling with his backpack, tuning me out. Glancing at him in the rearview mirror, I could see his eyes getting heavy. It made me happy to see him content and worn out from his day of fun.

I pulled into the driveway and turned off the car, unable to convince myself to park in the detached garage. It was easier just to pull up by the kitchen door. Truth be told, the garage was a tiny bit creepy, so dim and dusty, with boxes stacked along the walls and old tools scattered on a workbench.

"TJ," I gently rubbed his shoulder. "Go get cleaned up. Dinner will be ready in half an hour." I watched him clamber out of the car, and followed him up to the back door, bags of groceries in hand.

I set the bags on the kitchen counter and put away items that needed to be refrigerated, leaving things I needed for dinner sitting out.

"Alexa, set a timer for 10 minutes," I called as I dumped the bag of spaghetti into a pot of boiling water.

Timer set for 10 minutes, came the response.

Dinner was on the table by the time TJ came back downstairs, and I filled his plate with pasta and a bowl with salad. He did an admirable job cleaning his plate, but most of the salad was still in the bowl by the time he asked if he could be excused.

He scooted back upstairs after finishing his pasta, rinsing his dishes and putting them in the dishwasher.

I hummed to myself as I cleaned up the kitchen and turned on the dishwasher. Seeing my baby excited about something made my heart happy.

It was too early to get ready for bed, and the TV's guide didn't list anything I was particularly interested in watching. Not that I minded. I was content to curl up in the corner of the couch with my Kindle and a glass of wine. For almost the first time since Tom's death I was able to concentrate on the story I was reading, my mind not tied up in a knot of worry and grief. Funny, only two things had changed: I'd made a new friend and my son was looking forward to tomorrow.

When my eyes started to lose focus and I kept re-reading the same paragraph, I knew it was time to turn in for the night. I looked in on TJ, smiling at the small bundle under the comforter, a dinosaur book open on the floor by his bed. "I love you, honey," I whispered as I leaned over him and kissed his forehead, stifling a yawn as I headed for my own room.

"Alexa, set an alarm for six forty-five tomorrow morning."
Okay. Alarm set for 6:45 a.m. tomorrow morning.

Right on time, Alexa's blue ring lit up and a buzzy humming sound roused me from sleep. I stretched and swung my legs off the side of the bed, sitting up and rubbing my eyes, not bothering to ask Alexa to let me snooze for fifteen minutes. It felt like I'd turned a corner. I found the sunlight coming in the east window of my bedroom welcoming, instead of resenting its intrusion into my darkness.

I showered and dressed and roused TJ, then went downstairs to make breakfast before we needed to head for the church parking lot.

He jumped out of the car as soon as I stopped, tossing a "Goodbye, Mom" over his shoulder as he spotted Mike and Kevin standing by the bus.

"Bye, sweetie," I called, knowing he was already out of earshot. I smiled and shrugged as I pulled out of the parking lot.

It seemed like a good day to explore Marysville. The city exuded a New England vibe, with its century-old architecture and lush greenery. The downtown area was entrancing with its brick Victorian and Regency buildings, some dating from the 1800s, many with arched doorways and wrought-iron balconies. Inside, the aging but modernized buildings featured an array of quaint boutiques, antique stores and restaurants. Not a single "big box" store to be found. The fragrance of summer blooms in flower baskets hanging from old-time black-post streetlights wafted through the air, their sweet smell intoxicating. I felt good. How long had it been since I'd been able to say that?

The temperature hovered in the mid-80s. Hot and mid-level humid. Not miserable. Yet. Half a block down from where I'd parked, a cute boutique caught my eye and I stepped inside, sighing in appreciation of the air conditioning. Given the heat of late June, the summer selection of shorts and tank tops was especially enticing, and mostly on sale to make room for the upcoming fall season. After forty-five minutes spent browsing and trying on summer outfits, I left the store with my bank account $200 lighter. I walked along, swinging my shopping bag and looking in windows, now and then stopping when something caught my eye. In a few of the stores, I braved introducing myself, wanting to make connections, to make Marysville start to feel like home.

An antique rocking horse in a shop named *Dreams of Yesterday* caught my eye. I tried the door, and noticed the posted store hours indicated the store was closed on Tuesdays. Disappointed, I peered through the window for a few more minutes before I moved on, intending to try again in the future.

I think I fell in love with it. Growing up, I had a small collection of rocking horses. Two, to be exact. They currently reside in my parents' attic. If I'd had more room growing up, the collection might have been much bigger.

Now, I have more room and, maybe, just as much desire.

I probably can't afford it anyway, I thought, ruefully shaking my head. Even looking through the store's window, I could tell it wasn't your run-of-the-mill rocking horse. It was a gleaming chestnut-colored horse with real horsehair for its mane and tail, a leather saddle with stirrups, and deep brown glass eyes. I'd always wanted one of the true-to-life horse-hide covered rocking horses.

Before heading home, I stopped at Molly's Pie House and picked up a cherry pie for TJ, his favorite. I didn't let him eat a lot of sugary desserts, so this would be a treat.

The tart sweet aroma of the pie filled my car as I drove through the quaint tree-lined streets. Reminiscing over the day, I found myself smiling a genuine smile. It was good for me to get outside of my grief, and being out in the world was the way to do it.

Jen and I had lunch toward the end of the week. She'd made a list of vital contacts for almost anything I might need: plumbing, electrical, handyman, babysitter, house cleaner. I was set now.

We shared pictures on our phone; me of Tom and TJ, her of her fiancé Jason. They were childhood sweethearts who broke up after high school but found their way back together following college. Nice looking guy.

A couple of years younger than my 28 years, I found Jen to be very different from me in some ways. She was a little shorter than me. At 5' 7", I've always been taller than most of my friends. My hair is blonde, hers is dark brown, but long like mine. Those differences don't qualify as *very different*, though. Where she really differed is that, notably, she was bubbly and happy. I was not.

I was trying, though.

"I think I've forgotten how to let it all go," I said. Jen and I were sitting in the town's only Mexican restaurant, a dark, hole-in-the-wall establishment with the aroma of tortillas and roasting chili peppers permeating the air. "The grief, I mean. I used to be bubbly and sunny, like you, until Tom was killed. People used to remark on how much I laughed. I wish you could have known me the way I was. I just haven't gotten my equilibrium back yet."

"Kelly, it hasn't been that long since you lost your husband. You can't expect the sadness to go away with a snap of your fingers. You'll get there. Don't be so hard on yourself. Feel what you need to feel."

"I know you're right. I have to give it time. Maybe if I hang around with you enough, some of your exuberance will rub off on me."

Jen laughed. "I'm sure it will. I'll do what I can to help it along."

"I don't cry myself to sleep every night anymore. Puffy, red eyes and a headache were my morning reality for a long time. I still have bad days, just not as many."

"Sounds like you're making progress." She cleared her throat. "If you don't mind me asking, Kelly, can you tell me about . . . what happened to Tom?"

She caught me off-guard. It wasn't that I didn't want to tell her, but when the tears threatened, she noticed and apologized for asking.

"Sorry," I said. "I'm okay. Really. But maybe we should talk about something else for now."

"Of course. I'm really embarrassed." She looked alarmed at my reaction, which made me alarmed that I'd made her uncomfortable.

I wiped at my eyes with my napkin and leaned across the table toward her. "Is my mascara all messed up?"

She laughed and pointed to a spot under my right eye. "Maybe just a little right there."

I fished a mirror out of my handbag and dipped my napkin in my water glass, then proceeded to dab at the small spot. "Thanks," I said after I'd scrutinized my face.

I returned the mirror to my handbag, and cleared my throat. "About Tom," I started.

"It's okay. I don't mean to pry."

"You didn't. I just . . . . He was killed by a drunk driver. A stupid son of a bitch drunk driver."

"How awful." She reached across the table and touched my hand. "I can't imagine how you must feel."

"I feel a lot of things. Grief, loneliness, of course. But anger. That's the one that seems to consume me. I hate the man who killed Tom."

"I would, too." She sighed and took a sip of her iced tea. Neither of us knew what to say.

I wadded up my napkin and dropped it on the table. "You probably need to get back to work."

"Probably," she said. "But we should do this again. And I promise we'll only talk about fun things."

CHAPTER 5

On my way home from lunch, I noticed the door to the antique store was open, and impulsively pulled into a parking space. The horse looked at me from its prime spot in the window and I smiled. Once inside, I made a beeline for the horse, running my hand over its smooth coat.

"I can carry it to your car for you," a deep voice behind me said.

"Thanks, but I—" My voice trailed off when I looked up into the face of the good-looking man who'd spoken. "I, uh, I'm just looking." What was wrong with me, stuttering because of a man I just met?

"No problem. Glad you stopped in. I'm Rob Porter. Let me know if you have any questions."

"I will, thanks." I pushed my hair behind my ear and extended my hand. "I'm Kelly Harris. I recently moved to Marysville."

"Nice to meet you, Ms. Harris. How do you like our little town?"

"So far, so good. My son and I are settling in."

"Can I get you some coffee or a bottle of water?" He laughed. "Maybe it's a little warm out there for coffee."

"Water would be great. Thanks."

I watched him walk toward the back of the store. There was something about him that appealed to me beyond that he was handsome, quite handsome, although that didn't hurt. He had a genuine warmth about him, a welcoming vibe. I found myself wondering about him, whether he was married, had kids. Not that I was interested in that way. It's in my nature to be curious.

"Here you go," he said as he handed me the bottle. "I'll let you browse. Let me know if you have any questions."

I smiled and found myself following him with my eyes as he walked away. A tug in my heart brought tears to my eyes, as memories of Tom came unexpectedly. I'm not sure why. I think I felt guilty for having even one thought about Rob Porter.

A tissue from my pocket corrected the problem, and when my eyes were dry enough I turned back to the rocking horse, running my hand over its silky coat. It was even nicer in person. In almost pristine condition. I turned over the tag and tried not to gasp at the price. $1,500. From England in the early 1900s. Such perfect condition must mean that it hadn't graced the playrooms of little children.

A tad rich for my budget. Ah, well. I gave a short laugh. What would I do with it anyway? But I glanced back over my shoulder at it once more as I walked away.

I browsed among old furniture and various pieces of *objet d'art*, also known as knickknacks. There were lots of ancient tools and kitchen implements, glassware, dusty pictures in dusty frames. Now and then, I glanced around for a glimpse of the proprietor elsewhere in the shop. Not that it mattered. I wasn't open to anything, even if he turned out to be single.

Perusing a glass case, I picked up the lid of a small box with various rings and old jewelry tumbled together inside. I fingered through it all and picked out a round pendant that was no bigger than a quarter. It was an indeterminate gold or silver, with tiny diamonds or rhinestones and no chain. I found it pretty and intriguing, my mind wondering about its history. As Rob approached, I held it up and asked the price.

He laughed. "Just a dollar. A bargain, right?"

I laughed, too. That probably left out the possibility that they were diamonds, or that it was real gold or silver for that matter. "I think I want it. Do you know anything about it?"

"I don't know where it came from. Sorry. It's been in that little box for a long time."

I pulled a dollar out of my wallet and a quarter from my coin purse and handed it to him.

"Keep the quarter," he said with a grin.

"Let me know if that rocking horse ever goes on sale."

"Sure thing," he replied as I walked out the door.

Once outside, I glanced back over my shoulder. To be honest, I wasn't sure whether I was looking at the horse or looking for Rob.

JEN WAS HAVING A FOURTH OF JULY barbeque and invited me and TJ. I wasn't sure whether I would go or not. The fourth would have been Tom's thirty-first birthday. We always celebrated with sparklers on his cake. I didn't think I could spend that day with anyone else. Just me and TJ.

Jen had been excited when she invited me to her party, telling me about the themed foods she was making, the people she was looking forward to introducing me to. I should have told her then that I wouldn't be able to make it, but I didn't want to put a damper on her enthusiasm. Then I felt guilty, like I'd led her on.

Two days before the Fourth, I realized I shouldn't put it off any longer and texted to tell her I couldn't go to her party. She seemed disappointed, but I knew it was for the best. While I would have liked to meet more new people, I didn't want to try to make small talk when all my thoughts were with Tom.

TJ begged me to make a sparkler cake anyway. "It's a tradition," he said, his big blue eyes, so like Tom's, pleading with me. "I promise to help and even do dishes." We both knew his version of helping with the dishes would be licking the beaters. Still, I shopped for ingredients and sparklers while TJ was in camp.

The Fourth was Saturday and TJ was home all day. We spent the morning making Tom's special cake, which didn't take long given it's boxed Angel Food with chocolate whipped cream frosting. I'm pretty sure Tom picked chocolate for TJ's sake. As predicted, TJ sat on a stool and licked the beaters. He also got to stick the sparklers in, his contribution every year since he was old enough to put them in without ending up with frosting all over himself. After lighting the sparklers, I took some pictures of TJ's face next to the cake, a Happy Birthday Dad card on the other side.

From the front porch swing, over the tops of the houses, we could see faraway fireworks. We sat there eating our cake as we watched the bright, colorful explosions. It was bittersweet. TJ and I each tried to hide our sadness from the other, but I knew, once we retreated to our rooms, we'd each give in to the grief that still had us firmly in its grip.

CHAPTER 6

July fifth dawned sunny and bright. And hot. I peered in the bathroom mirror at my red-rimmed puffy eyes. I needed a couple of teabags to reduce the swelling. TJ wasn't up yet, and I made my way to the kitchen as quietly as I could, being careful not to wake him.

Minutes later, I was again lying in bed with the damp bags on my eyes. It had been a painful night, filled with thoughts of Tom, of how big the hole was he'd left behind in my heart, of how much I missed him. I'd hugged my pillow, trying to pretend I was holding Tom. That only made it worse. But this morning, I would put it all aside. Tom wasn't coming back and I had to go on living. For TJ *and* for myself.

I gave myself half an hour for the teabags to work, then peeled them off my eyes and carted them into the bathroom to toss. I examined my face hopefully. It wasn't as bad as it had been earlier. It would do.

I hummed a little as I brushed my teeth and stepped into the shower, scrubbing my shampoo-laden hair and rinsing off coconut-lime soap, feeling refreshed.

Wrapping my hair in a towel and pulling on my terry-cloth robe, I stuck my head in TJ's room, finding him still asleep.

Good. That meant I had time to dry my hair and dress before I needed to start breakfast.

I was surprised I felt as good as I did. Maybe all the tears had cleansed the grief from my heart. At least for a little while.

By the time TJ ambled downstairs, I had scrambled eggs and bacon warming on the stovetop.

"Hi, honey," I said. "Hungry?"

"Um hm," he said, rubbing his eyes.

"You okay?"

"Dot was crying last night," he said through a yawn.

"Dot? Who's Dot?"

"You know. Dot. Alexa's Dot."

I stared at the back of his head, frowning, as I dished up his breakfast.

"Alexa can't cry. Are you sure you didn't imagine it?"

"Mom. I'm eight. I'm not a kid anymore." He looked at me with a scowl. "I don't imagine things."

"Tell me exactly what happened, then." I slid onto the chair opposite him at the table with my own plate of food and gave him my full attention.

"My light was off. Well, except for the night light. And I was thinking about camp on Monday. That's when I heard it."

"Heard Alexa?"

"Yes. It sounded like this." He made an exaggerated sobbing sound.

"But how do you know it came from Dot?"

"Because I told her to stop and she did."

"That's strange, all right, sweetie. I can't imagine what it was, but call me next time it happens so I can hear it, too."

He nodded as he stuffed a piece of bacon in his mouth, apparently tired of talking about it.

I thought about TJ's odd story while I finished breakfast and stacked the dishes in the dishwasher, then forgot it as I dialed Jen's number to apologize again for missing her party.

"We missed you!" she said, a smile in her voice. "People wanted to meet you."

"Sure they did," I said with just the right amount of skepticism. "It was … the Fourth is Tom's birthday, and I needed to be with TJ."

"Oh, I'm sorry. No wonder you didn't want to come to a party. It totally makes sense."

"Thanks for understanding. We had a cake to commemorate the day. It wouldn't have been right to not honor it, at least this first year. But today's another day, and TJ and I are going to the town square to see if anything's going on there today. Any chance you want to meet us there?"

"What time are you going?"

"In an hour or so. I want to do something fun for TJ."

"Sounds great. I can't wait to meet him."

THE TOWN SQUARE WAS BUSY with people celebrating the Fourth of July weekend. Booths decorated in red, white and blue lined the street, selling everything from T-shirts and jewelry to artwork and knickknacks, along with several food vendors who kept the revelers well-fed. Jen found us by the hotdog booth chowing down on holiday fare that we normally made a wide berth around. TJ had a hotdog—plain, of course—and potato salad. I'd loaded my plate with a burger and fries. And a ton of ketchup. Jen slipped onto the picnic table bench opposite TJ and smiled warmly.

"That looks good," she said to TJ. "Do you recommend it?"

He nodded vigorously and gulped the bite of hotdog. "It's great! Don't put that goop on it, though. That ruins it."

"He means mustard and relish. He hasn't progressed to condiments yet."

"I don't like them, Mom," he retorted.

"I know, sweetie. Maybe someday you will, though."

He shook his head as he took another bite, sure that day would never come.

"The burger's pretty good, too," I said. "Go grab something and come have lunch with us."

Jen headed for the burger grill and was back at our table in no time, plopping down next to TJ.

"The town square is really fun on holidays. I'm glad you're here to experience it," she said to TJ before turning to me. "After we eat, I'll introduce you to a few of the locals. I know just about all of them."

We sat enjoying the sun, which hadn't reached insufferable yet. Jen glanced at TJ, and said, "How's summer camp going? Your mom said you made some new friends?"

"It's cool. I like the hiking. I hope we see bears!"

"Please, God, no!" I said. "Thanks for putting that idea in my head."

Jen laughed. "We don't see a lot of those around here. But, who knows, maybe you'll get lucky."

"That would be the best thing ever!" TJ's face radiated with excitement at the possibility.

"Come on." She bumped him with her shoulder. "Let's explore the festivities."

We stopped at almost every booth in the park, and Jen introduced me to the person manning each one. She wasn't kidding about knowing just about everyone in town.

TJ suddenly perked up and waved. "Mom, there's Mike and Kevin!" He looked at me over his shoulder for permission, and rushed off to join his friends.

"Let's go say hi to their parents," Jen said. "If you haven't met them yet, I'll introduce you."

A small group of people sat on blankets, a couple of coolers holding down the edges, and the boys gamboled nearby.

A woman who seemed a little older than me waved and invited us to join them. She moved over, making room for Jen and me on the blanket.

Jen leaned over and gave her a hug. "Melissa, this is TJ's mom, Kelly. I thought you should all meet since it appears your kids are fast friends now."

I greeted Melissa and she motioned toward another woman sharing the blanket. "Sherry, this is TJ's mom, Kelly."

"I love your outfit, Kelly" Sherry said, indicating my white cotton shorts and light blue short-sleeved top.

I laughed and made a little curtsy, not easy from a sitting position. "Thanks. It's courtesy of one of the cute shops on Main Street."

"I'm pretty sure I know which one. Love shopping there."

In a few short minutes I'd met Melissa and Sherry, their husbands, and a few other friends. My little circle seemed to be expanding. It was nice to lounge around in the afternoon sun. I felt almost normal again.

"LET'S GO CHECK OUT THE SIDEWALK sales." Jen stood and pulled me up from my spot on the blanket. "It's okay if TJ hangs out with you guys for a little while?" she asked Melissa, who smiled and waved us off with a "Sure."

We browsed the boutique where I'd previously dropped $200, and I managed to find a white cotton eyelet sleeveless shift dress and cemented the store's position as being my future go-to spot for whenever I needed to find something cute. I picked through a tray of accessories while Jen paid for the shorts and T-shirts she'd picked out.

As we passed the shoe store half a block down, Jen grabbed my arm and dragged me inside to point at a pair of white sandals she thought would be perfect with the outfit I'd just bought.

"It's a good thing you work for a bank," I said. "I might need a loan if we keep finding things I need to have."

She laughed. "I've got you covered."

When we passed the antique store, the skin horse stared longingly at me through the front window. Or maybe it was me with the longing look. "Let's go in here," I said, turning in the door.

I glanced at the counter, searching for Rob, but an older woman was minding the store. She waved a hi to us, asking if she could be of help.

I started to say no, but then approached her. "Do you have any chains?" I pointed at my neck. "Maybe a longish one?"

"We do." She pulled a tray out of the glass display case. "Here are a few. Are you looking for gold, silver, what?"

"I want it to go with this." I dug in my purse searching for the pendant. My fingers closed around it and pulled it out. I opened my hand to show her.

"Oh, you bought that pretty piece. I didn't realize it was gone."

"I did. It just spoke to me somehow. The guy who was in

here sold it to me for a dollar. I hope that was all right?"

"Oh, Rob. Yes, of course it was all right. I'm glad it found a home." She smiled as she lifted a silver chain. "How does this one do?"

I set the pendant on the counter next to the chain. "Let me try it on." I threaded it through the pendant's loop and fastened it around my neck. "What do you think? I asked, turning to Jen. "Is this too long?"

"No, I like that length, and the pendant looks great on you. You look very elegant wearing it, with your long blonde hair falling around your shoulders." She comically wiggled her eyebrows.

I gave her a playful shove. "I guess I'll take it," I said to the saleslady with a laugh. "I don't need a bag. I'll wear it. Since my friend thinks it makes me look elegant."

She smiled and rang up the sale, and I handed her my Visa. As she handed it back to me, along with the slip to sign, I asked, "I don't suppose you know anything about the necklace? Rob didn't know where it came from."

"Actually, I found it while hiking up in the Red Creek Range. It was in the path, and I accidentally kicked it and it glinted in the sunlight, otherwise I wouldn't have seen it. I brought it back and cleaned it up. As far as where it was before it wound up on the hiking trail, I have no idea."

"Oh, well, that's more information than I had before. I really like the pendant, and I'm glad you had a chain so I can wear it."

"I'm glad you like it. I'm Gina, by the way. You're a friend of Jen's?"

"I am, lucky for me. I'm Kelly."

"Why, thank you," Jen said, nudging me with her elbow.

"Well, I'm glad to meet you, Kelly," Gina said. "I hope you'll stop in here to browse every now and then."

"I'm sure I will. I came in here the first time to look at that rocking horse in the window."

"Isn't it wonderful? It needs a good home, in case you know of any." She winked.

"I'd love to have it. Who knows? Maybe one of these days, if it's still here, I'll decide I can't live without it."

A smile crossed her face as she gave me a knowing nod. Jen and I waved goodbye and headed back to the town square. I wanted to pick up TJ and stop at the market on the way home.

Jen gave TJ a hug. "I used to babysit your new best friends, you know."

"Really?" He looked up at her shyly. "I wouldn't mind if you want to babysit me, too."

"I don't really do that anymore, but you never know. Maybe I will sometime."

I looked at TJ. I think my son had a little bit of a crush on my new friend.

CHAPTER 7

A frightened "Mom" roused me from a fitful sleep. I swung my legs off the bed, the hardwood cool against my feet. "I'm coming," I called as I rushed to TJ's room. I found him sitting up in bed, his eyes big and worried.

"What is it, sweetie?" I asked as I sat beside him. "Did you have a bad dream?"

"Mom, Alexa was crying again."

"What do you mean?" I tipped his face up and looked him in the eyes. "Alexa can't cry. She's not a real person. Tell me what happened."

"I was asleep and I heard a little girl crying. There wasn't anybody in my room but I could still hear it."

"Maybe you were dreaming."

He crossed his arms over his chest and glared at me. "I wasn't dreaming, Mom."

"Okay, then. Maybe it just sounded like crying."

"There were words, too."

"Words?"

He nodded. "I said, 'is anybody there' and the crying

PAMELA MCCORD

stopped. Then Alexa said *Help us*." His serious eyes dared me to not believe him.

"Let's ask her," I said. "Do you want me to ask Alexa?"

He nodded, wide eyes watching me.

"Alexa, are you crying?"

No. I'm not crying. Maybe it's raining . . . in the cloud.

"Alexa, is someone in there with you crying?"

I don't know that one.

"See, honey. It wasn't Alexa."

"But I heard it." He turned his face away from me. "You don't believe me."

"Honey, I believe you heard something. I'm just not sure what it was. Do you want me to sleep in here with you tonight?"

"Yes."

"Okay, let me turn off the light." My fingers were on the switch when an item caught my eye and I paused.

"TJ, why is my necklace on your dresser?" I picked it up and showed it to him.

"I don't know. Why would it be in my room?"

"I left it in my room. How did it get here?"

"I didn't take it. I don't know why it's here."

"There are only two of us in this house. I didn't bring it to your room, so you must have. I'm not mad, honey, but I want you to tell me the truth."

There was no mistaking the hurt in his eyes. "I didn't do it, Mom. Honest."

· 48 ·

He looked like he was telling the truth. I'm pretty good at reading my son, and I would swear he wasn't lying. Confused, I shook my head and turned off the light. "Okay. No problem."

I climbed in beside him and pulled the covers up over his thin shoulders. He rolled on his side and I draped my arm over him. I didn't know what was going on in here, but I intended to make sure he wouldn't be afraid the rest of the night.

I think we both slept well, and if Alexa sobbed her little heart out, neither of us heard her.

In the light of day, the odd experiences didn't seem so urgent, but I'm not gonna lie. The events from the night before worried me. Twice TJ thought he heard crying in his room. What would cause that? And I was more than a little concerned about the incident with my necklace. I knew I hadn't taken it into his room, and he insisted he didn't touch it. I'd never known him to lie to me, and he didn't look like he was hiding anything. But nobody was in the house except us. If there was a logical explanation for what was going on, I wanted to hear it. Until then, I had to wait to see if anything else was going to happen. There were enough other things to deal with, and I didn't want to dwell on it.

After I dropped TJ off at the Methodist church parking lot, I decided to treat myself to a mocha at Jane's Special Coffee. Jen insisted that the locally-owned coffee shop would beat anything I'd had in a big city. The day having already reached eighty-four degrees, the cool interior of the coffee shop was a welcome respite, and the smell of freshly roasted coffee beans was heavenly. I ordered a mocha and moved out of the way of others waiting to place their orders. Based on the crowd, I was thinking Jen must be right about the quality. When my name was called, I collected my coffee and pushed through the door, nearly colliding with Rob Porter on his way in. Only his hands gripping my bare shoulders prevented me from crashing into him.

"I'm so sorry," I said, surprised. "That was close. I almost spilled my mocha all over you."

A hint of red tinged his face as he dropped his hands. "Are you okay? Ms. Harris, isn't it?" He smiled sheepishly. "Nice to see you again."

"I'm glad you can say that after I almost ran you down."

"I'm still alive and not covered in coffee," he laughed.

"That's only thanks to your lightning-quick reflexes."

"Do you have to rush off? Why don't you join me for coffee?"

I hesitated, uncomfortable at the thought of being alone with him. Before I could answer, he said, "It looks nice on you."

"Excuse me?"

My puzzled expression led him to add, "The pendant. It looks nice."

"Oh." My hand flew to my neck, my fingers closing around the necklace for a moment. "Thank you. I got this chain at your shop, too. It's perfect."

He indicated a table and raised his eyebrows.

"I, uh, I really can't. I need to run a few errands before I meet a friend for lunch."

Was it my imagination that he looked disappointed? "I better run. It was nice almost running into you."

A smile highlighted the laugh lines around his eyes. "Maybe next time."

"Yeah, maybe," I said, turning away. After a few steps I felt the urge to look back. When I did, he was watching me. Embarrassment at having been caught as I turned to look heated my skin, and I wondered if he was as embarrassed to be caught as I was?

It wouldn't be right, I argued with myself about whether I should have stayed. *He's not Tom.*

Of course he's not. I'm not looking for another Tom. I was irritated with myself at not being able to put Rob out of my mind. I shook my head to clear it and to remind myself that there wasn't room in my life for a complication like Rob Porter.

I sipped my mocha, troubled that I'd given one thought to Rob, a man I'd barely met, and so soon after losing Tom. Guilt rushed over me. I knew I shouldn't feel guilty for thinking about another man. I even knew that Tom wouldn't expect, or want, me to stay alone for the rest of my life, but the feeling of uneasiness was real. It made me want to run home and crawl under the covers and shut out the world.

I texted Jen that I couldn't meet her for lunch after all,

then got in my car and headed for home. I had to be alone to think. To sort out the confusing thoughts that a few innocent words with Rob Porter had caused.

"ALEXA, SET AN ALARM FOR FOUR this afternoon," I said when I walked into my bedroom.

Alarm set for 4 p.m. today.

I contemplated the tall black cylinder that housed the computer-generated voice that answered to its name. "Alexa, can you cry?"

Boo hoo. Oh, wait, boo ya.

I gave a short laugh. Of course she can't cry.

I plopped down on my bed, then rolled onto my side and curled into a ball, my hands fisted at my eyes. *I'm sorry, Tom. I miss you so much. I'll never forget you; I'll never get over you. I'm sorry, Tom.*

I let the tears fall, saying over and over how sorry I was, how lonely I was, how everything would never be all right again. But the guilt stayed.

I must have dozed off, because I jumped when I heard Alexa's insistent buzz/hum thing.

"Alexa, stop the alarm."

After a big stretch to wake all the way up, I wandered into the bathroom to splash water on my face before I left to pick up TJ.

I passed Jane's Special Coffee on the way to the Methodist

church parking lot, and found myself glancing at the door. *He remembered my name.* I wonder if that means—

Stop, I commanded myself. You don't care about Rob Porter. He probably remembers the names of all his customers. You don't need to think about Rob Porter. But I glanced at my guilty face in the rearview mirror. *Stop.*

CHAPTER 8

Jen was already waiting at Molly's Pie House when I arrived the next day. As we followed the hostess toward our table, I noticed a MISSING CHILD flyer tacked to the hostess stand. A picture of a little girl with big eyes stared at me. My heart ached at the thought of what her mother must be going through.

"Did you see that flyer about the little girl?" I asked Jen as I sat down opposite her. "How awful for that family."

"I know. She's been missing for a few weeks. The police don't have any idea what happened to her."

"Do you know her?"

"I know her parents, although not well. Her name's Marilee Harmon. I think she's six."

"I hope somebody finds her, and I hope it's not too late."

The server stopped to get our beverage order and, since we knew the menu backward and forward, we ordered our lunch at the same time.

"I'm sorry I cancelled yesterday. I was feeling under the weather." Though Jen and I have been developing a strong friendship, I wasn't ready to share the complexities of my jumbled emotions. She didn't need to know that 'under the weather' was code for 'emotional meltdown.'

"Are you okay today?"

"Yeah, it was nothing. Oh, I meant to tell you about the weird thing that happened at my house."

"What weird thing?"

"TJ claims that Alexa is talking to him."

"Well, that's what Alexa does," Jen said, a teasing glimmer in her eye as she popped a French fry into her mouth.

"No, I mean, he said she was crying. It's happened twice and freaked him out."

"Honestly, it kind of freaks me out, too. What did you do?"

"I told him that Alexa can't cry. I'm not sure he believed me."

"Do you believe him?"

I sighed. "It doesn't make any sense, but it sure seems like he thinks it happened. And my necklace." I fingered the pendant. "It was in his bedroom, but he said he hadn't touched it. I'm sure I left it on my dresser before I went to bed. Nobody's in that house but the two of us. So . . . weird, huh?"

"Gotta admit it's strange. I guess you have to wait to see if it happens again, unless you want to sit up and watch Alexa all night."

"He said she also said, 'Help us.'"

"That gives me chills."

"Me, too." I fought against the shiver running up my back. "I'm sure it's nothing. I doubt it'll happen again."

"Maybe you have a ghost."

An uneasy and forced laugh escaped me. "I'm pretty sure my house isn't haunted."

CHAPTER 9

"I have plans for Saturday night. I accepted after Jen assured me I could trust Megan, the babysitter she recommended. She said you'll love her because she's a ton of fun."

It would be the first time I had left TJ alone since we moved to town, and I was concerned he'd be unhappy.

"Jen's having a little dinner party . . . a barbeque . . . and she invited me. You don't mind if I go, do you, TJ?"

"No, Mom. It's fine if you go have fun. You don't have a cool camp to go to."

I smiled and gave him a hug. *My little man.*

JEN AND I HAD BEEN FRIENDS for more than a month and I hadn't met her fiancé, Jason, yet, so I looked forward to Saturday. Thankfully, it was going to be a casual barbeque and I could dress comfortably in my favorite jeans, a nice pair that looked just a little bit upscale, and a lightweight summer top that went great with the jeans.

Jen said she didn't want me to bring anything since all of the food and drinks were being taken care of by Jason and her. When I said I wouldn't feel right showing up without bringing anything, she agreed I could bring TJ's favorite chocolate chip cookies. I think the real reason she relented was because she was afraid TJ wouldn't be thrilled about me leaving him with a babysitter and figured fresh-baked cookies might offset his disappointment.

After dinner and the getting-ready-for-bed routines were out of the way, I bid TJ goodnight with a hug and a kiss before he trudged up the stairs to his room. Later, as I passed his partially open bedroom door, I heard him say, "Alexa, tell me a bedtime story."

I smiled. TJ learned early on that she could tell a variety of stories and, he'd often request an Alexa one once he was in bed with the covers pulled up to his chin. I stopped and poked my head in to say goodnight before heading for my own room.

WHIMPERING WOKE ME AROUND three. I sat up and listened but didn't hear anything more, so I slipped back down under the covers and closed my eyes. Until I heard a loud "*Mom.*"

I swung my feet off the bed and slipped on a robe before I headed for his room. As I opened my mouth to speak, I heard crying. "Honey?" I said, sticking my head in the door. One more sob stopped me, and then another. I could swear it came from the Alexa Dot. I looked at TJ and he pointed at it. I walked slowly past the Dot, not taking my eyes off it.

"See? I told you, Mom," he whispered.

I didn't know what to think. The Alexa was silent, but I knew I'd heard it crying, the same as TJ had heard several times before.

"What's it doing, Mom?" TJ looked at me for an answer I didn't have. Instead, I crossed to the dresser where the Dot was sitting. Waiting?

"Alexa, what—" I stopped when I saw my pendant draped at the base of the unit. Glancing over my shoulder, I said, "TJ, what's my necklace doing in here? Did you take it?"

"No, Mom. And I didn't take it before, either."

I wanted to believe him. There was nothing about my little boy that indicated he was lying to me. He'd never told more than a little fib before. Why would he now?

"I don't know what's going on, honey, but it's okay. You need to go back to bed." My mind was spinning, but I didn't want TJ to be any more freaked out than he already was.

"Will you stay with me?"

I sat on the end of the bed, unable to take my eyes off Alexa. Giving TJ a small smile, I said, "You can sleep in my room tonight."

Come morning, I was reluctant to open my eyes. The troubling events of the previous night replayed in my mind. TJ would have questions for which I didn't have answers.

He came downstairs as I was stacking pancakes on a plate for him. I could feel his eyes on me and gave him what I thought was a reassuring smile as I poured syrup over the stack.

"Mom, does Alexa talk to everybody like that?" The look in his trusting eyes tore at my heart.

"I don't know, honey, but we'll figure it out."

He bent his head as he cut a bite from the stack of pancakes.

"TJ, I don't think you should talk to people about this, okay? I mean, they might not understand."

"Mom, *I* don't understand."

"Neither do I, sweetie. That's why I want to keep it between us for now, okay? Hurry up and finish so we can get you to camp."

"But what about Kevin and Mike? Can I tell them?"

I considered it a moment. "I'd rather you didn't. At least for now. I don't know how they'd take it, and they'd probably tell their parents, and pretty soon it would be all over town. So, can you not tell them, please?"

He nodded slowly, but I could see the disappointment on his face.

I dropped him off, and did a little marketing. Once back home, I stood in the kitchen staring at my to-do list. My mind kept wandering back to the night before. Abandoning my list, I went up to TJ's room and stood watching Alexa. I picked it up, examined it and saw nothing unusual. I returned it to the dresser and sank down on TJ's bed. It had been so weird.

The doorbell disturbed my reverie, and I tromped down the stairs and opened the front door.

"Kelly Harris?" a youngish man asked.

"Yes. Can I help you?"

He handed me an envelope. "You've been served."

He turned and walked away before I could think quickly enough to say anything. I stood there dumbfounded, my eyes following him as he climbed into a faded maroon Toyota Corolla and drove away.

I carried the envelope into the kitchen and poured myself a cup of strong coffee before sitting down at the kitchen table. Taking a deep breath, I opened the letter and read over it. "My God, I'm being sued," I said out loud. The plaintiff was one of Tom's cousins, Tara Edley. *What the Hell?*

She wanted the house. My house. I stared into my coffee for a few minutes, not believing the turn of events. I took a sip and set the mug down. What was that lawyer's name? The estate lawyer who'd notified Tom about his inheritance? Jeff something. Tilting my head, I searched my memory. I'd looked over the papers from his office when Tom first learned about the house he would get from his grandmother's estate. Jeff Silver. That was it. Now all I had to do was look for the paperwork regarding the inheritance.

It only took five minutes. Thanks to Tom's keen sense of organization, his files were neatly packed in boxes which I'd stacked in one of the empty bedrooms. If I hadn't been stressed out over the lawsuit, I might have patted myself on the back for having been careful when I moved Tom's important papers instead of shoving them willy-nilly in the garage. I was able to find the separate file he had set up for his grandmother's will fairly quickly.

Luckily, the lawyer was local and I was able to make an appointment for Monday. Thinking about the lawsuit weighing on me over the weekend made my stomach clench. I felt crappy about the whole thing.

CHAPTER 10

I'd promised TJ he could help me make cookies for the barbeque on Saturday morning. I left my rings and necklace upstairs on my dresser and put on an old T-shirt and an apron to avoid getting cookie dough all over me. I let him measure ingredients, stir the sweet mixture and lick the beaters, and told him he could watch TV while the cookies baked. He popped into the kitchen pretty quickly after they came out of the oven. I couldn't blame him. The smell was hard to resist for me, too.

I sat down with him and we both had two cookies and a glass of milk before I cleaned up the kitchen.

I almost changed my mind about going to Jen's barbeque, but decided I could fret with a glass of wine at a party as well as I could with a glass of wine sitting by myself in the front room of my house. *My* house.

I SHOWED UP AT JEN'S SATURDAY afternoon with cookies and a case of beer. The front door opened before I had to juggle the cookies and beer to knock.

A handsome dark-haired man I recognized from the pictures on Jen's phone grinned at me. "You must be Kelly." He noticed the case of beer and said, "Let me get that for you. Come on in. Everyone's out back."

"Thanks. It was getting heavy." I smiled at the warm welcome I saw in his eyes.

I followed him into the kitchen, where he set the beer on the counter, then took the plate of cookies from me and set it down as well. Sticking out his hand, he said, "I'm Jason, Jen's fiancé."

He nodded toward the patio doors and I thanked him again and made my way toward the small group gathered in deck chairs.

Jen noticed me and waved. Other heads turned. One of those heads was Rob Porter's.

He smiled and stood to grab a chair, pulling it into the group area and raising his eyebrows to inquire whether I would join him.

I blinked and shuddered inside, feeling unsure for a heartbeat, then made an imperceptible shake of my head to get back in the game, and smiled back.

Jason appeared at my back to find out what he could get me to drink. I asked for a white wine and took the seat Rob had offered. At first, nervous, I scolded myself that I was a big girl and a little social interaction wouldn't kill me.

"We keep running into each other, don't we?" he said.

"We do," I agreed with a smile, feeling a warm blush and hoping it didn't show on my face.

Jason strolled back, handing me a glass of wine and one to Jen before he sat down next to her. I enjoyed watching her eyes twinkle when she looked at her fiancé. Until that twinkle morphed into an inquisitive spark when she turned her attention to Rob and me.

"So, how do you two know each other?"

Taken aback, I opened my mouth but nothing immediately came out. Rob seemed to take it in stride. He sipped his beer and said, "Kelly came into the shop to ogle the antique rocking horse in the window."

"I know that rocking horse," Jen said. "She always wants to stop and see it."

"I do not," I protested with a grin. "I admit I like it, but TJ's too old for a rocking horse." I turned to Rob. "I don't ogle either."

He laughed. "You might as well admit it. You want it for yourself."

"I think you're right, Rob," Jen said.

Being a gracious hostess, she let me off the hook and introduced me to the other couple, her neighbors from next door. Randy and Georgie Baker were older, maybe in their late 40s. Georgie had brilliant red hair that clouded around her face, held back on one side by a barrette. Randy was stocky and muscular, with thick brownish silver hair. He seemed jovial and extended a large hand to shake mine. I liked both of them immediately.

Maybe noticing my reticence, Rob didn't laser in on me. My nerves started to come under control as I sipped my chardonnay, although I was always aware of him sitting to my right.

When Jason nodded toward the barbeque, Rob stood and walked over to join him. Rob poked at the charcoals with a long fork while Jason went inside, returning with a platter of burger patties and hot dogs. I couldn't help myself. My eyes were drawn to Rob. I took a gulp of my wine to still the guilty warning voice telling me *too soon, too soon.* My mouth tightened and I sighed. *I know it's too soon. I'm still in love with Tom and that's not going to change.*

But Rob stood there, jeans sitting low on his lean hips, a long-sleeved black T-shirt with a faded flag on the front and "U.S.A." down one arm. The shirt fit just snugly enough to showcase his biceps and strong shoulders. His stomach was flat and I envisioned a muscular six-pack. He glanced at me to catch me watching him. I turned away, caught, and silently cursed myself. *I'm not interested in Rob.*

I didn't even know if he was interested in me. He'd been polite and friendly, but that didn't mean he was looking for a relationship or anything. I'm a customer. He *has* to be friendly.

"I think Rob likes you," Jen said later as we stood side by

side in the kitchen slicing onions, tomatoes and lettuce for the burgers.

"Oh, no. I doubt it. Besides, I'm not ready to date yet. I don't know if I ever will be."

Then I felt the words spill out, but I couldn't stop them. "Besides, surely he has a girlfriend or something?" I wanted to kick myself. I splashed more chardonnay into my glass and quickly took a couple of sips.

"He doesn't. Not because women aren't interested. Believe me, he's definitely an eligible bachelor. A *gorgeous* eligible bachelor. He's just not looking. You're the first person I've seen catch his eye in a really long time. So, if you should decide . . . ." She let her voice drop off.

"Oh, I don't think so. Tom's only been gone a few months. It wouldn't be right."

"Please. It wouldn't be right for you to lock yourself up in an ivory tower and pine away for your lost love." She recoiled at my stunned look. "I'm sorry, Kelly. That came out more blunt than I intended. I get it that you're still grieving. You're the only one who'll know when you're ready. It's just . . . Rob's a nice guy. A great guy. Just a little info to tuck away for future reference."

She picked up a tray with buns and another with the sliced tomatoes, onions and lettuce leaves, while I grabbed the condiments and we carried them out to the redwood table, setting them on the end closest to the barbeque. I glanced up to find Rob looking at me. He smiled when he caught my eye. I smiled back. *I'm so confused. And the wine isn't helping.*

I leaned toward Jen. "Have you told him about me? About . . . what happened?"

"No. I didn't know you two knew each other. Besides, it would be against the Girl Code to share your personal information."

"Oh. Okay, thanks."

Jen, Georgie and I were urged to start the food line. I moseyed up to the cook and held my plate out for him to lay a burger on the bun I'd dressed up the way I like it and thanked him before sliding onto the redwood bench at the far end. I was busy squirting an obscene amount of ketchup on my plate (I need it to be on every bite of my burger) and didn't notice when Rob sat next to me. I probably blushed, but managed to sheepishly offer him the bottle of ketchup.

"Sorry," I said. "Despite appearances, I really didn't use all of it."

His face lit up with a big grin. "No problem. Personally, I like to be able to taste the meat, but that's probably just me."

I concentrated on my burger, trying not to be aware of Rob sitting next to me. It kind of worked for a while, until he offered to refill my wine glass, which, of course, opened the door to actual conversation.

He was easy to talk to, and I found I was enjoying myself. When the food had been whittled down, Jen and Jason began the clean-up process. Georgie and I offered to help, but Jen waved us off and disappeared into the kitchen. Georgie found a seat on Randy's lap and the two of them got a little *involved* with each other. When Rob suggested adjourning to the deck chairs, I agreed, relieved that maybe I wasn't the only one uncomfortable with the PDA. I moved so quickly I almost turned my chair over when I got up. Rob grabbed the back of the chair to steady it and flashed an understanding grin.

He carried our drinks and led the way.

"Have you always lived here?" I asked.

"Born and bred. I was born at Marysville General. My parents lived their whole lives here."

"Are they still in Marysville?"

"No. Unfortunately, I lost them both in the last few years."

"I'm sorry to hear that."

"It's okay. I've had time to deal with it." When he glanced at me, I thought I caught a momentary twinge of grief around the edges of his gaze, but it was gone so quickly I might have imagined it.

"Do you have any brothers and sisters?" I asked.

"No. I was an only child." He smiled wryly, looking at his hands.

"Me, too," I said. "About being an only child, I mean. I still have my parents. Other than TJ, they're about the only family I have left, although there's an aunt in Connecticut."

"What made you decide to move to Marysville?" he asked after arranging our chairs next to each other.

I glanced away, not answering immediately. When I turned back, he was watching me, a concerned look on his face. "I'm sorry," he said. "I don't want to pry."

"It's okay," I said. I took a deep breath. "My husband inherited the house from his grandmother."

"Your husband?"

"Yes. His name is . . . was . . . Tom. He died a few months ago."

He sat back abruptly, obviously not expecting my answer. "I'm sorry," he said again. "I didn't know."

"I know. How could you? He was killed by a drunk driver. And that was the end of our family. Not really, but it felt like it." I shouldn't have told him all this, but he was so easy to talk to. He felt safe. I glanced down at my hands that were wrapped around the bowl of my wine glass and shrugged. "Tom inherited the house when his grandmother, Kate, passed away. Maybe you knew her?"

He cleared his throat. "Oh, sure, everyone did. Are you doing okay out there by yourself?"

"I'm not really by myself. I have a son, TJ. He's eight."

"I'm glad you're not alone. Are the two of you settled in?"

"Pretty much. There are a few boxes left that I haven't done anything with. Kate left us the furnishings and all the kitchen stuff, so there wasn't a lot we brought with us, mostly clothes and personal things. It's a lovely house and we're really lucky to have it." I took a sip of my wine. "It was hard being in our old home. It was just an apartment we rented in New York, but there were memories. Lots of memories. In a way, it was good that we had somewhere else to go, as it was sad there, at home." I looked down as the unexpected emotions washed over me.

It must have showed on my face because he put his hand over mine. For a moment, I welcomed his touch but, when I looked into his eyes and saw the compassion there, I felt like I couldn't breathe, and I pulled my hand away.

"I'm sorry. I didn't mean—"

"No, I'm sorry. I guess I'm just not ready for . . . anything. Not that you meant anything by it." I stood. "I should go. I need to relieve the babysitter. It was nice talking with you," I said abruptly as I walked away. At the doorway, I glanced back to find him watching me, looking confused. I gave a small wave and disappeared inside to say my goodbyes.

Guilt roiled my stomach, almost causing me to hunch over in physical pain. *I'm sorry, Tom. I love you. Only you.*

I set my still-almost-full glass of wine on the counter and made my apologies to Jen. She protested, but gave up when she realized my mind was made up, and hugged me before I stepped out the door.

Sitting in my car, the dam holding my emotions in gave way and hot tears poured down my cheeks. I surrendered to the waves of guilt and grief for a few minutes, then squared my shoulders. I didn't do anything wrong. I was confused that I felt drawn to Rob. I shouldn't. I couldn't. But a little voice in my head asked *why not?*

CHAPTER 11

Turbulent emotions kept me awake. At two thirty, I gave up trying to sleep and padded downstairs to make myself a cup of tea. I sat in the dark kitchen, moonlight streaming in the window over the sink my only companion. I sipped and contemplated. Eventually the warm comfort of the tea calmed my shaky nerves and I headed back upstairs. I poked my head in TJ's door, tiptoed in and sat at the foot of his bed watching him sleep.

A chill came out of nowhere. I glanced at his window, but it was closed and locked. I bent over him and pulled the covers up around his shoulders. That's when I heard sobs that seemed to echo around the room. I whirled my head around but no one was there. I started for the door, but it slammed shut as I approached. A small cry escaped me and my hand flew to my mouth. My hair lifted around my face as if a wind swirled through the room, and I froze. And, then, something impossible to believe happened. Alexa said *Help us* and a child's eerie crying filled the room.

"What the hell?" I turned the doorknob and pulled, but

the door wouldn't open.

"Mom?" TJ sat up in bed. I could see his wide, startled eyes in the light from his nightlight, and rushed to his side.

"We have to get out of here," I whispered, a tinge of urgency coloring my voice as I helped him out of bed.

Please, the disembodied voice said. *Help us.*

The door banged open. Grabbing TJ's hand, I pulled him out of the room. We flew down the stairs and huddled in the living room.

"Mom?" TJ was scared and confused. He'd slept through most of the strange events, but he could see that I was frightened, and that frightened him.

I was breathing hard and had to take a few deep breaths to calm myself down.

"What's wrong, Mom?" he asked fearfully when I still hadn't spoken.

"It's okay, TJ." I finally managed to speak with a voice that wasn't quivering. I hugged him, not sure whether it was to comfort him or me, and said, "Everything's okay. We're going to go out for a while." We could find a hotel for the night and figure everything out in the morning. If only I didn't have to go back upstairs. Where my clothes and my car keys were. But I was the adult and had to protect my son, although the choice between taking him back upstairs with me and leaving him alone in the front room stumped me for a moment.

In the end, I decided he would be safer with me, so I held

his hand and led him back upstairs. I couldn't help glancing toward his empty room as we passed it, but hurried on to my own room. I quickly changed into my jeans and a T-shirt and grabbed a hoodie, a duffel bag and my purse. I tossed my toothbrush and a spare for TJ into the duffel, along with a few other things I thought we'd need in the morning. There were clean clothes for TJ in the laundry room, sparing me the scary thought of going back into his room.

"Was it Alexa?" he asked, rubbing sleep from his eyes as we climbed into my car.

"I don't know, sweetie. I'm not sure. We'll find a nice hotel so Alexa or whoever it was won't bother us."

A BELL OVER THE MOTEL DOOR tinkled as we entered. The desk clerk stepped up to greet us, trying to look pleasant in spite of his bleary eyes and disheveled appearance. He was probably dozing in the hopes that no guests would be arriving after midnight.

I apologized for the late hour and handed him my credit card. TJ stood next to me and I draped an arm over his shoulders, pulling him next to me in a semihug. Silently, I signed the credit card slip and accepted the key to a first-floor room. The desk clerk automatically asked if I needed help with my luggage, and I automatically said no as I indicated the duffel bag at my feet.

TJ was fading fast. I couldn't blame him after being dragged out of his bed in the middle of the night like that. I guided him down the hallway to a room next to the elevators.

Dropping the duffel bag on the round table just inside the door, I closed my eyes and thought about how I could explain what had happened to TJ. When I turned around, though, he was already curled into a ball on one of the queen beds, the covers pulled up almost over his head. He looked so small and innocent. In the morning, I had no doubt he would have questions.

CHAPTER 12

When the sun came up, I rubbed my eyes and stretched, then remembered where we were. I dropped an arm over my eyes and listened for TJ, but all was quiet on his side of the room.

What was I going to tell him? How was I going to explain it when I didn't understand it myself? I took a deep breath and shoved up into a sitting position. We'd work it out.

By the time I was out of the shower and dressed in my jeans and T-shirt, the sound of cartoons emanating from the room's TV signaled that TJ was up. I ruffled my damp hair with the towel and sat down on my bed. "Hey, buddy. You hungry?"

"Um, yeah."

"Go brush your teeth and get dressed, then we'll go to Molly's. Sound good?"

He nodded on his way to the bathroom. I finished towel-drying my hair and used my wide-toothed comb to tame the tangles.

I'd already stuffed our few items in the duffel bag, then

added TJ's pajamas to the bag when he brought them out.

We dropped the room key off at the front desk on the way to the car.

Shortly, we were seated in a booth at Molly's Pie House. The bench seats were shiny red vinyl, and chrome poles held up the Formica tabletop. When I was a kid, we'd search the swirling patterns in the Formica for monkey shapes. Through the years, we'd found those same shapes in Formica tabletops in our friends' homes. The monkey shape right in front of me triggered the memory, and I absently traced it with my finger as a cup of coffee was placed in front of me.

"I have one, too, Mom." TJ pointed out his own monkey shape.

"What are you looking at?" Anita, our server, asked.

"They're monkeys. See?" TJ said with a smile.

"I never noticed those before," Anita said. "How cool is that?"

"It's fun to find them," he said.

Anita took our order and swept away from our table, her pink cotton uniform skirt brushing against the monkey table as she turned.

"So." I looked at TJ, wondering how to start the conversation. He watched me expectantly.

"I know last night was probably scary," I began.

"Huh?" The confused look on his face confused me.

"You know, when we had to leave and go to the motel?"

"Oh, that. That wasn't scary."

Apparently, he had missed or forgotten the whole Alexa thing. Or he was getting used to it. I supposed it was best to leave it that way. "I guess not," I said. Was I wrong? Had anything even happened? In the light of day, the things that frightened me last night seemed impossible. I guess I should be glad that TJ wasn't traumatized.

A breezy "Hi, Kelly" caused me to look up to find Jen and Jason smiling down at me.

"Hey, you guys," I smiled back.

"We just came from church and are going to have breakfast then hang out in the square. Want to join us?"

I wasn't dressed for socializing, but it would be good to take my mind off whatever had happened last night. "We'll go change after we finish and meet you there," I said.

"Great," Jen said and waved as she and her fiancé headed for a table on the other side of the room.

"Does that sound like fun to you?" I asked TJ, who nodded vigorously, a big grin on his face.

"Then, eat up. We have to go home and change."

WITH TREPIDATION, I PUSHED open the front door and stood listening. No sound. The house felt normal. How could it? Something strange had happened here last night. TJ pushed in past me and flopped on the couch. I looked at him and then at the staircase, and decided he should stay downstairs. I turned the TV on and said I was going to go change.

I walked as quietly as I could up the stairs and stopped outside TJ's door. With a deep breath, I stepped inside. Nothing was out of place and the Dot stood silently on the dresser. "Is anyone here?" I asked hesitantly.

Nothing.

No breeze lifted my hair, no cold temperature, no sobbing. I rubbed my arms to calm my nerves, then picked out a folded T-shirt for TJ, watching Alexa the whole time I was going through his clothes until I closed the dresser drawer.

With relief, I shut the door behind me and crossed to my own room. By then, I was starting to doubt my recollection of last night. Could I have imagined it? I didn't think so, but . . . well, I didn't suppose I could rule that out.

JEN AND JASON WERE SITTING on a blanket close to the bandstand and we headed toward them. TJ spotted Mike and Kevin and asked if he could go play with them. I made him say hi to Jen and Jason first, and watched after him as he ran off in the direction of his friends.

"Are you okay?" Jen asked, startling me back to the present. "You seem a little . . . off . . . this morning."

I glanced at Jason and back to Jen. "It's nothing," I said.

"Does it have anything to do with last night?" she said. "You left early and—"

I felt myself flush. "No, your party was great. I just thought I needed to go so the babysitter could get home."

Jen looked skeptical, but didn't say anything.

"I have a lot on my mind," I said. "We can talk about it later."

"No problem. Do you want a water?" She pulled a bottle out of her cooler and tossed it to me.

"Thanks. Listen, I'm sorry about last night. Tell me what happened after I left."

"Not a lot. Rob left shortly after you did, and Jason and Randy and Georgie and I sat around drinking and eating. You missed dessert by the way."

"What did I miss?"

"I made a cherry pie. It was amazing if I do say so myself."

"I can vouch for that," Jason said, slipping an arm around Jen's shoulders.

"My favorite! Actually, so is pecan pie and chocolate cream pie. Just off the top of my head."

Jen laughed in response and took a sip of her water. "It's gorgeous out today. Perfect for hanging out at the town square. I think there's going to be music later."

"Cool." I was starting to relax.

"Rob was afraid he might have offended you," Jen said.

"What? Oh, my God. No. I'm afraid I offended him. He was just being a nice guy." I sighed, feeling a hint of tension in my neck. "I sort of panicked. I'm not used to, you know, a man paying attention to me. Since Tom, I mean."

"I told him that was probably what it was."

"Should I say something to him?"

"Only if you want to."

I kind of did. "I owe him an apology. I'll tell him if I see him again."

"It's a small town. Trust me, you'll see him again. Besides, he's fine."

Thoughts of Rob had been shoved aside by the middle-of-the-night events. Now I couldn't help thinking about him, about how nice being with him had been. A cloud of guilt floated toward me, but I pushed it away. I didn't have to feel guilty. Tom wasn't coming back, and he wouldn't want me to close myself off from life. I pictured Rob, his kind, expressive eyes, his broad shoulders. The way his mouth . . .

That was going too far. I shook myself. *No. I'm not ready for that.*

I stretched my legs out in front of me, luxuriating in the warm breeze swirling around the square. I didn't want to think about anything at the moment. The weekend had been stressful enough, and Monday would be spent with the estate attorney. More stress. For the moment, I just wanted to bake in the sun.

But thoughts came anyway. Of Tom . . . and of Rob. It was too soon. I couldn't possibly be interested in another man. Rob had been so kind last night, so interested in me. So sympathetic when I told him about Tom. Then he touched me. It was silly of me to run away like that.

I didn't do anything wrong. I wouldn't feel guilty for being in the same room with him, or for liking the feel of his hand on mine. I'd try not to feel guilty about the way I ran away from that same room. Not room. Backyard. Semantics . . .

I opened my eyes and glanced toward the sound of boys playing. TJ looked happy. It made my heart warm to see him with his friends, laughing and carefree.

When would I be that way again?

CHAPTER 13

Late afternoon brought the aroma of grilled hot dogs and hamburgers into focus. The food booths had been there all day, but until you're hungry they don't register. We were all hungry. TJ begged for money, which I gave him, along with a request for him to bring a burger back for me. Jason offered to go with TJ, leaving me and Jen alone for the first time all day.

"Okay, spill. What's going on with you?" she asked. "Should I be worried?"

I shrugged. "TJ and I spent last night in a motel."

"What?"

"I think I have a ghost problem."

Her mouth dropped open. "No you don't!"

"Maybe I do."

"Tell me what happened."

"Remember I mentioned that the Alexa in TJ's room talks? And cries?"

"Did you hear it?"

I nodded. "It was so weird."

"What does it say?"

"It said, *help us*."

"Help who?"

"I don't know. I didn't hang around long enough to question it."

"Are you pulling my leg?" Her eyebrow quirked up.

"I wish I were. But, unless I'm losing my mind, I'm serious."

"But what—" The return of Jason and TJ with food ended our conversation.

"We can talk later," I said as TJ handed me my burger, along with packets of ketchup and a bunch of napkins.

It had been hours since breakfast and all of us were starving. Nobody talked while we stuffed our faces, but I could feel Jen watching me.

We didn't get a chance to talk again. At six, a local country western band started playing and claimed everyone's attention. Jen was swaying to the music and singing along, but my thoughts were all over the place and I couldn't concentrate. After half an hour, I decided to leave. Jen gave me a hug and said to call her if I needed anything. Then, holding me at arm's length, she asked if TJ and I wanted to stay at her house.

Her offer was sweet and generous, but I told her we'd be okay. I hoped I was right.

While TJ took his bath, I visited his room. Nothing seemed out of the ordinary. I sat on his bed and waited for something, anything, to happen. I said "Are you there?" to Alexa but it didn't respond. I wasn't sure what was more troubling, that she didn't answer or that I thought she would. Had I imagined the events that had me dragging my 8-year-old out of the house in the dead of night?

Everything seemed normal. I stood at the window looking out. It wasn't fully dark yet. The house stood on a forested lot, and usually the view of the trees from the window comforted me, but tonight I was too keyed up, ready to jump at any sudden noise.

"Mom, what are you doing?" TJ asked. He was in pajamas, his hair wet and spikey. I smiled at him.

"Just enjoying your view. Are you ready for bed now?"

"Yeah. Can I read for a while?"

"Sure." I cleared my throat. "Do you want to sleep in my room tonight?"

"Nah. I like my room best. Do you want to sleep in my room?"

I laughed. "It's a nice offer, but I guess I like my room best, too. But call me, okay, if you get scared."

I pulled the covers up around his neck and kissed his forehead, my pulse racing at leaving him alone in his room.

He mumbled a "'Night, Mom" and curled up on his side with a book. My cue to leave.

Opting against pajamas, I pulled on leggings and a sweatshirt. Just in case.

With the nightly rituals of brushing my teeth and washing my face out of the way, I climbed into bed and lay still, listening. For a long time. But there were no sounds except the creaking of an old house.

More than once during the night I tiptoed into TJ's room. All was well. No sounds other than the rhythmic breathing of a deep sleep. I carried a throw and settled into the antique rocking chair occupying a corner of his room, keeping a watchful eye. Until I didn't. The sun coming in his window woke me and I stretched, suddenly noticing where I was. I felt peaceful. There'd been no voices during the night. A cautious optimism settled in that maybe the night before had been nothing more than a quirky turn of events.

CHAPTER 14

I was fifteen minutes early for my appointment with Mr. Silver. His law office was in a historic building near the town square. The building had been upgraded in recent years, but still bore the musty scent of age. Whoever did the remodel had done an excellent job of capturing the original design of the interior while adding modern touches to support current technological needs. Still, the dark wood and leather the designer had employed lent a certain gravity to the law office.

The receptionist sat at a large mahogany desk and was working at her computer when I walked in and announced my appointment with Mr. Silver.

She smiled and escorted me to a small glassed-in conference room off the reception area, offering me something to drink. I declined her offer and instead pulled out my cell to check messages.

Jen had texted about getting together for lunch. As I finished texting her *yes*, the conference room door opened.

"Ms. Harris? Very pleased to meet you," Mr. Silver

greeted me with a smile and an outstretched hand, and took a seat opposite me. "I was sorry to hear about your husband. Very tragic."

I thanked him with a solemn nod.

He cleared his throat. "How may I help you?"

I pulled the summons from my handbag and handed it to him. "I think she wants my house."

He scanned the document silently for a moment.

"Can she do that?" I asked.

"Well, she can certainly try," Mr. Silver said. "I believe Kate's will was specific, and that she was of sound mind. I have no reason not to believe that." He flipped open the file folder he'd brought with him and searched through it for a minute or two. "Here's Kate's will. There were only a few bequests. The largest one, by far, was the house, which went to your husband. She left Tara Edley $20,000 and another $20,000 went to Daniel Prentiss, a nephew. She also left a sum to a charity for abandoned animals." He read through it again. "Her bequests were specific, not a general division of her estate. This should bolster your case."

"Why?"

"Because it shows she had a definite idea of how she wanted her property divided. I don't really foresee a problem for you. I'll attend the court hearing. At this point, I don't think there's any reason you would have to be there."

I felt relief and smiled tentatively. "That's good to hear."

"If there's nothing else," he stood, "I'll get started on this. Please call if you have any questions."

"Thank you," I said, gathering up my handbag. "I appreciate your help."

My appointment with the lawyer had gone quickly and there was more than an hour until lunchtime. With the rare extra time, I took a walk around the town square, finding myself peering in the *Dreams of Yesterday* window, the horse peering back at me. I wandered inside, hoping to see Rob, but Gina was the only one there.

I was disappointed. I owed him an apology, but it would apparently have to wait.

"Your horse is waiting on you," Gina said with a smile.

I laughed. "Does everyone think I need that horse?"

"Apparently. Don't you?"

"I don't know. My resolve slips a little bit every time I come in here." I wandered around the shop. "I'm meeting Jen for lunch in a little while so I'm just killing time." Realizing what I'd just said, I apologized. "That didn't come out right. I *meant* that it's always fun to browse around in your store."

Gina laughed. "You're always welcome. Buy something, don't buy something. I'm glad to have people stop in. Let me know if you find anything you just have to have."

"I will," I said. I was curious where Rob was, but managed to restrain myself. No sense giving anyone the idea that I might be interested in him. Of course, I wasn't. That would be inappropriate.

PAMELA MCCORD

Jen texted that she was ready for lunch. I texted back that I'd meet her at the Italian restaurant a block away from the bank where she worked and a short walk from the antique store.

As soon as we were seated, Jen pounced. "Tell me everything!"

"Everything?"

"The *ghost*?"

"Oh, that." I shivered. "Well, it *could* be my imagination running away with me."

"Maybe you should start at the beginning."

"Strange things have been going on in that house. First, TJ told me he heard Alexa crying. While I was in his room, I found my necklace on his dresser. I already told you about that." I fingered the pendant. "He insisted he hadn't brought it in there, and I certainly hadn't taken it off in his room. So, there was that."

"Um hmm. And what else?"

"The next night, I heard TJ yelling for me. He was scared. He said Alexa talked to him. He said she said 'Help me.'"

"Now I'm scared!" Jen said with a shiver and a smile. "Is that why you spent the night in a motel?"

"No. It was what happened after your party. Unable to sleep, I went into TJ's room to check on him. It suddenly got really cold and then I heard it, too. It was Alexa, and she was crying. Then the door slammed shut and I couldn't get it to open and there was wind swirling around the room. Scared me to death. Then, Alexa said *Help us*, and TJ woke up. The voice said *Help us, please* and started to cry and then the door flew open. I grabbed TJ and dragged him out of the room." I took a gulp of my water. "That's when I packed up and TJ and I spent the night in a motel."

Jen looked stunned. She didn't say anything; just stared at me for a long moment. Then she shivered again and said, "Oh, my God."

I shrugged.

"What are you going to do?"

"I don't know. We stayed at home last night. I ended up spending half the night dozing in the rocking chair in TJ's room, but nothing happened. So, did I imagine everything?"

"It would be kind of hard for a person to imagine all that. And you don't seem like someone who would. And, don't forget, your son heard it first."

"You're right. He did."

"Oooh. You have ghosts!"

"How is that even possible? It sounds like my house is haunted, doesn't it?"

"It kinda does. I don't have any experience with haunted houses other than from movies. Do you want me to come over and stay one night to see if anything happens?"

"Thanks, but it hasn't been happening every night so you might not hear or see anything. I appreciate the offer, though."

"Is it okay to say I'm relieved you said no?"

I laughed. "I don't blame you."

I picked at my Caesar salad. "Besides, I have something else to worry about."

"What's that?"

"I'm being sued."

"What! By whom? Why?"

"One of Tom's cousins is disputing the will. She thinks Kate's house should have gone to her."

"That sucks. Are you going to talk to someone?"

"I met with the attorney who handled Kate's will this morning. He thinks the will is sound and told me he'd take care of it."

"I hope he's right."

"Me, too. I can't help worrying, though."

"Hello, ladies," a voice sounded over my shoulder.

"Hi, Rob," Jen said, looking past me.

"Rob?" I turned my head to say hi. I don't know why, but I was surprised to see him in a gray suit. His tie was loosened and the top button of his white shirt was open. "You look so different."

"Why don't you join us?" Jen asked. He looked at me, a question in his eyes.

I slid over in the booth and he hesitated a moment and sat beside me.

"I don't want to interrupt your lunch," he said.

"You're not. I have half an hour before I need to get back to the bank. Plenty of time for you to order and have a bite with us."

The server appeared and looked at him expectantly.

"Can I get a submarine sandwich?"

"Coming right up, Rob," she said with a smile.

"What's going on?" he asked Jen.

Her eyes glinted mischievously. "Kelly was just filling me in on some excitement in her life." I shot her a look and she quickly said, "Just kidding. Her life's about as exciting as mine." She glanced at me and quirked her head. I took it to mean that she wanted me to talk to Rob.

The server set a cup of coffee in front of him. He thanked her as he pulled the cup closer, grabbed the creamer and sloshed a little in his coffee, and looked at me over the top of his cup as he took a sip. I squirmed and smiled and cleared my throat.

"You're kind of dressed up to work in an antique shop," I said.

He laughed. "I don't actually work there. I was covering for my aunt while she ran an errand that day."

"He's a cop," Jen said.

I looked at him. "Really? A cop?"

"What, you don't like cops?"

"I didn't mean . . . of course I like cops. I *love* cops." I knew I was starting to babble so I picked up my water glass and took a gulp. And started coughing as the water went down the wrong pipe.

Jen and Rob both laughed. I'd have laughed, too, if it wasn't me doing the coughing.

Jen looked back and forth between Rob and me. I could

practically see the cogs turning in her brain. She was up to something. I was almost sure of it.

"Sorry to bug out on you," she started as I glared at her, "but I forgot I have a meeting with my supervisor and I don't want to be late. You guys have fun." She opened her handbag, left some money on the table, and stood. I think she knew I wasn't pleased with her because she flashed a smile at Rob but barely waved at me as she scooted out of the booth.

An awkward silence stretched between us until the server arrived with Rob's sub. He'd moved to the other side of the booth after Jen had left to give me more room, thanked the server and picked up the sandwich. "Excuse me. I'm just gonna—"

I made a small laugh. "No problem. I have my salad to finish." For several minutes we ate without speaking.

I looked up as I took a bite of my salad to see a concerned look on his face. He cleared his throat. "I'm sorry about, you know, if I was too—"

It caught me off guard, and my heart sank, the heat of embarrassment creeping up my neck. I lowered my eyes, unable to hold his gaze. I'd almost forgotten about the apology I needed to give him.

"You weren't too anything, Rob. You were a perfect gentleman. It was me. I suppose I've been a mess since losing Tom. I completely overreacted. It's me who owes you an apology."

"No apology needed. I'd never want to make you

uncomfortable. I know you're still grieving. It's just ... I like you. No strings or anything. I just think you're someone I'd like to get to know better. If, you know, you feel like you'd like to get to know me better, too."

I didn't have an answer for him. My feelings were too tangled up. The best I could do was smile at him and gulp my water. Carefully this time.

After a moment, I looked at him and smiled tentatively. "How long have you been a policeman?"

"Detective, actually. Ten years. More or less."

"Isn't Marysville a pretty quiet town?"

"Pretty much. Not a lot of violent crime, mostly B&Es and vandalism."

"Oh, that's good to know."

"Yeah."

I think he was as uncomfortable as I was. He was done eating but the server had just refilled his coffee, otherwise I might have made an excuse to go. Since he had his coffee to drink, I would have felt awkward leaving abruptly. Again.

My emotions were confusing. I was scared and wanted to bolt. I was excited to be with him and wanted to stay. I felt guilty for not honoring Tom's memory.

I squared my shoulders. I could do this. I told him I might like a cup of coffee so he flagged down the server and had her bring me one.

The mundane actions of opening the sugar packet and dumping it in my cup, pouring in creamer and then stirring was comforting and helped calm my jitters. I picked up the warm cup and sipped my coffee.

"I saw some posters around town about a missing little girl?" I said.

"Yeah, Marilee Harmon. It's a tough case. Her parents are devastated."

"I know I would be if anything happened to TJ. So, no leads or anything?"

"Not anything I can talk about. You know, ongoing case and all."

"Oh, sure. I understand."

He picked up his cup but didn't drink from it. "Anything new with you?"

"No. Yes. No."

He chuckled. "Now there's a straightforward answer for you."

"Sorry about that. Some strange things have happened lately."

"What strange things?"

Was I really going to tell him about Alexa? "Yikes. You wouldn't believe me if I told you."

"That's intriguing. You have to tell me now." He sipped his coffee and set down the cup. "If you want to. I don't want to pry. I remember what happened last time."

"Oh, God. I'm really sorry about that. That was all me being . . . something. I don't know what was wrong with me, jumping to conclusions that way." I was making it worse. "I mean, I didn't jump to any conclusions. I didn't think you were coming on to me or anything." *Shut up. Just shut up.*

"I wouldn't—"

"I know you wouldn't, you know, do anything that was—" I could feel my cheeks burning. "What in the world are we talking about?"

"Should we try for neutral ground?" he asked, folding his hands in mock seriousness.

"Yes, please."

"Anyway, you don't have to tell me anything you don't want to."

"I appreciate that. It's just, it's kind of weird, and you'll probably think I'm crazy." I took a deep breath, then another one. "I think my house is haunted."

He laughed, then stopped himself. "Wait. You're serious?"

"I don't know for sure. I mean, who can be sure about something like that? But it's unnerving."

"Huh. Can you tell me what exactly happened?"

"I guess. Do you know what Alexa is?"

"Alexa? Sure. I don't have one but I've seen them in friends' houses."

"You know that if you want to ask them something you say *Alexa* first?"

He nodded.

"That's how you turn them on. Anyway, our Alexa has been crying."

"Crying?"

"Yes. And it also said *Help us*."

"No kidding? What did you do?"

"The night of Jen's party is the last time something happened. The door to TJ's room slammed shut when I was in there and I couldn't get it open and Alexa was crying and asking for help. As soon as the door opened, I grabbed TJ and we spent the night in a motel. We moved back yesterday and nothing happened last night. You probably think I'm a crazy person now."

"Well, I wouldn't go that far," he said with a grin. "A little out there maybe."

I raised my eyebrow. "You're making fun of me."

"I know. I'm sorry." He looked sheepish. "What are you going to do?"

"Nothing for now. Just wait to see if it happens again. And keep my fingers crossed."

"Well, call me if it happens again. I'll come over and see if we can figure out what's really going on."

"I don't want to bother you."

"It's no bother. If it happens, don't wait for morning. Call me and I'll be there in five minutes. Or, if you want me to do an inspection to see if there's anything out of place or unusual going on, I can do that, too."

"Ghost hunting isn't really part of your job description, is it?"

"No, not really. But helping a friend is."

"Are we friends?" I felt a flush creep up my neck and

made a show of picking through the remnants of my salad.

"I certainly hope so." He took a sip of his coffee, and glanced at his watch. "Whoa. It's getting late. I need to get back to work. Sorry to rush out on you." He took another gulp of his coffee and set the cup down.

"Sorry if I made you late."

"It's okay. I'm not on the clock but I have several cases sitting on my desk needing my attention." He tossed a twenty on the table. "Maybe I'll run into you again soon and you can let me know how your ghost problem is going."

"Maybe. Hopefully there won't be anything to tell." I turned and watched him walk out of the restaurant, suddenly aware that I was watching him walk out of the restaurant.

CHAPTER 15

With grocery shopping and a couple of errands checked off my to-do list, I headed home. Once the groceries were put away, there was no more stalling. I took a deep breath and went up to TJ's bedroom. I stood at the door looking in, taking a read on the room, before I sat down on his bed. I needed to figure out just how much of a problem I had. I sat in silence for a while. A long while. Shaking off my fears, I cleared my throat and said, "Is anyone here?"

The only sounds greeting me were the creaking of an old house.

"What do you want?" Still nothing, except I think I felt the temperature drop and I shivered. "Is anyone here?" I waited a minute more, then stood. "This is ridiculous."

I left TJ's room feeling no closer to figuring out what was happening than before I'd gone in. I couldn't help recalling Rob's offer to come check things out for me, and I smiled wistfully. Apparently, there was nothing to see here.

And I fervently hoped it stayed that way.

I picked up TJ from camp, watching him get off the bus

laughing with his friends, a big, blissful smile on his face. He was still smiling when he climbed in the car and regaled me with a description of how long he could hold his breath underwater. Longer than Mike or Kevin. I congratulated him, but couldn't help tossing in a warning to be careful in the water. It's a mom thing.

While I got the salmon fillets out for dinner, TJ was tasked with washing vegetables and whisking the balsamic vinegar, olive oil and lemon juice for salad dressing. If I let him help with the preparation, there was less chance he wouldn't want to eat whatever I served. Fish had never been a favorite of his, and it was only in the last year or so that he stopped crossing his arms and pouting when I *forced* him to eat it.

I let him drizzle melted butter over the salmon and sprinkle on herbs. I also let him add lemon slices and capers before he sealed the fish in tinfoil and put it in the oven.

The little cutie kept peeking through the oven door every few minutes. This was the first time we'd collaborated on salmon. When it was within five minutes of being done, I asked TJ to set the table while I took the fish out of the oven. He hovered, waiting for me to peel away the tinfoil.

"Doesn't this look good?" I asked.

"Yum. Can't wait."

"Go sit down and I'll bring it in, okay?"

I dished up the steamed broccoli and nestled it and some rice beside the salmon on the plate. TJ might be excited about the dinner, but I was practically salivating over the aroma.

Dinner tasted even better than I'd anticipated. It was the perfect distraction from all the stress. I needed a peaceful moment before facing the night and what it could bring.

TJ wasn't the slightest bit fazed over the pending evening. I asked him if he was okay sleeping in his room and he rolled his eyes as if I was being silly. I hoped maybe I *was* being silly. I could live with that.

After tucking TJ in for the night, I poured myself a glass of wine and disappeared into my own room. The warm comfort of the wine blunted the prickly worries I tried not to notice as I read a cozy paranormal romance novel on my Kindle. By ten o'clock, I was dozing.

"Mom!"

I jolted up in bed, disoriented for a moment. My instincts sent me rushing down the hall to TJ's room. "It's back," he whispered. I sat on his bed and pulled him into my arms. My eyes searched the dim room before landing on Alexa.

"What happened?" I asked him.

"She was crying again," he said, looking like he might cry, too. "Make her go away."

This was ridiculous. We couldn't ... wouldn't ... be chased from our house by something we couldn't even see. I kicked myself for not taking that thing out of his room after the first time, but TJ wanted it to stay so he could listen to his bedtime story.

I squared my shoulders and said, "What do you want? Do you need help? You have to tell me what you want."

The room was suddenly freezing. "Are you here?" I asked.

Help us.

I clenched my teeth, my mouth pressed into a thin line. "Tell me what you need."

Help us.

"Who are you?"

It seemed like she wouldn't answer, but after a minute, she said, *Emma.*

"Emma?"

I'm scared.

TJ was tugging on my T-shirt, his big eyes reflecting his fear.

"It's okay, TJ. She's talking to us. Maybe she can tell us what she needs and she can go away." He looked uncertain but didn't argue.

"Emma, tell me where you are?"

Again, there was a long spell of silence before she answered. *I don't know.*

"Are you alone?"

No. Marilee is here, too.

Why was that name familiar? I'd heard it before but couldn't place it. The crying started again and no matter how many times I tried I couldn't get Emma to talk to me again.

"Come on, honey," I said to TJ. "Come sleep in my

room. I'll talk to some friends tomorrow and see if we can figure out what to do. Okay?"

"Okay." He clambered out of bed and I took his hand and led him out the door and down the hall to my room.

I tucked him in and waited with him until he fell asleep, then I padded downstairs to put the coffee on, all thoughts of sleep erased.

WHEN THE SUN HAD COME UP AND it was late enough, I texted Jen to see if she wanted to meet for lunch, then went upstairs to check on TJ. He was sleeping peacefully, so I left him alone. Checking my phone, I saw that Jen had replied that it wasn't a good day for her. I waited awhile, wondering if it was a mistake, but finally texted her again to ask for Rob's phone number.

True to form, she made some smart ass comment akin to *Kelly and Rob sitting in a tree . . . .* But she gave me his number.

You think you're funny, don't you? I responded.

I AM funny. Seriously, why are you calling him?

She'd probably pester me until I told her all the details. Now wasn't the time, though, so I texted, *If we were having lunch, I'd probably have told you all about it. Sorry. You'll just have to wait.*

I needed to think about it more, however, before I would decide to call him. Getting TJ up and ready for the day was the perfect excuse to stall.

After dropping him off for camp, I stopped in at Jane's Special Coffee. I felt the need for a little comfort. As I sipped my mocha on the way out of the shop, I noticed the poster taped to the door, and suddenly I knew where I'd heard the name Marilee. She was the missing child. I almost choked on my mocha.

What could it mean that Alexa was talking about Marilee? And who was Emma? No matter how unlikely, I now had a valid reason to talk to Rob. Once I reached my car, I texted him that I needed to talk to him when he had a chance.

He responded almost immediately. *Did something happen last night?*

Yes. And it's something I think you might find interesting. Can you do lunch today?

If we do it early. I have a busy afternoon. Can you meet me at Molly's at eleven thirty?

Sure.

Relief at talking about my experience of last night mixed with the embarrassment of it being a ghost story. If Rob didn't think I was nuts before, this new information might seal the deal. I left my car where it was parked and walked over to the square with my coffee. A warm summer breeze rustled the leaves of the elm and maple trees dotting the park, and I found a bench under one of them so that I could watch the leaves dancing to the music of the wind. And turned my face into the gentle breeze. I'd always liked windy days. I just didn't like winds swirling through my son's bedroom.

I had a little time to kill before I needed to go to Molly's. I could visit my favorite boutique and poke my head in some of the other shops I hadn't explored yet. It seemed easiest to hang out in town until it was time to meet Rob. Anxiety kept me company while I waited until it was time to go.

CHAPTER 16

I got to the restaurant first, but Rob arrived before I was shown to a table. He smiled when he saw me and I thought he meant to give me a hug, but he apparently changed his mind and stepped back. He smiled sheepishly as we found a seat by the window.

Once the server had taken our drink order and had gone, Rob said, "I'm happy you texted me. I didn't know I'd get to see you again so soon."

I smiled and took a breath. "It's not really a social call."

"I know. You said something had happened last night?"

"Unfortunately, we had another visitation."

"Tell me about it."

"I can't believe I'm sitting here talking to a detective about ghosts. This must be a new one for you." I was thoughtlessly shredding my straw wrapper.

"Well, it's right up there." He took what was left of the straw paper away from me and gave me a reassuring smile. I let out a breath I didn't know I was holding.

"Seriously, you can tell me anything and I won't think you're crazy."

I gave a small laugh and cleared my throat. "The reason I thought I should talk to you is because of something the ... ghost ... said. It started with tears, as before, so I decided to see if I could communicate with it. It kept saying *help us*, so I asked what it wanted and if it could tell me its name. At first, I didn't think it would answer, but then it said Emma. I asked where she was but she didn't know." A shiver ran up my spine and I began to fold my napkin into smaller and smaller squares, not meeting his gaze. Rob watched my hands, but didn't try to stop me. "Her voice ... it was a little girl's voice ... it sounded so scared. She said she was scared. So, I asked if she was alone. This is the part I think you'll be interested in. She said Marilee was there, too."

Rob jumped like I'd slapped him. He didn't say anything, just stared at me.

"At first, I didn't know who Marilee was, but I saw that poster at Jane's Special Coffee this morning and I remembered where I'd heard the name. What do you think?"

His eyes grew hard. "Are you fucking with me?"

"Am I what?" I was surprised by his hostile reaction. "You think I'd make something like this up?"

"I don't know what you might do. I barely know you."

His words were like a punch to the gut. For a long moment I sat there, unable to move. Then I stood and grabbed my handbag, oblivious to the staring faces turned our way. "I'm sorry if you think I wasted your time. And I'm *really* sorry you think I'd lie to you." I slung my bag over my shoulder, shrugged my shoulders at the voyeuristic diners and stomped out of the restaurant. A moment later, I heard quick footsteps behind me.

"Wait," he said, taking my arm.

Too angry to listen, I jerked my arm away and stood for a moment trying to recall where I'd parked, then started off to the left. "Wait," he said again.

But I didn't. I rushed away from him, and he didn't follow.

When I reached my car, I slumped in the front seat, hot angry tears coursing down my cheeks. I was a fool to think he'd believe what I said. I was ashamed and my skin tingled with embarrassment and confusion at his reaction. For a second, I'd felt relief thinking I might not have to face this alone.

I found a napkin in the glovebox and dried my eyes and wiped my face, straightened my back and headed for home. "Oh, Tom. If only you were here. You'd believe me."

I threw myself into housecleaning until it was time to pick TJ up from camp. I wanted my mind to be occupied with something besides the sadness and anger that threatened to settle over me. And I wanted to get some of the aggression out of my system before my son came home.

Jen texted to ask how lunch with Rob went. With little smiley face emojis at the end.

Not well. He's an insulting mean jerk.

What??? He's not! You must have misunderstood.

He said the F word while he was insulting me. I hope for his sake I don't run into him again anytime soon.

Kelly, I can't believe he'd fly off the handle like that. What happened?

He called me a liar to my face. That's what happened. Anyway, it's not worth wasting my breath over.

Are you all right? Should I come over?

No. I'm okay.

You don't sound okay.

I'm dealing with it. I'll be fine.

I just can't believe he'd talk to you like that.

Are you calling me a liar too?

Of course not. You don't lie.

Thank you. I've gotta go pick up TJ soon. Bye for now.

I was surprised at how getting that off my chest helped. But it did, and my blood pressure was back to normal by the time I picked TJ up at the church.

Once again, he had seemed to shrug off the events of the prior night. He looked carefree and happy as he waved goodbye to his friends and hopped in the car.

"Let's pick up a pizza on the way home," I said, unable to face cooking.

"Yeah!" Pizza. His favorite food. At least *someone* still liked me.

It was a quiet evening. I was still under a cloud from my meeting with Rob, surprised at how much it upset me. But not really. No one wants to be attacked for something they didn't do.

We were done with the pizza when Rob texted, asking if

he could call me. I didn't respond. What was there to talk about?

CHAPTER 17

I sent TJ up to get ready for bed around eight thirty. A glass of wine was what I wanted. Something to take the edge off, maybe help me think more clearly about what to do about bedtime. I poured a glass of chardonnay and carried it to the living room, picked up my Kindle and sipped the wine.

A knock on the door startled me. I wasn't expecting anyone and it was after dark. I cautiously flipped on the porch light and peeked out the side window, taken aback to see Rob standing there.

I felt a flash of anger, but took a deep breath and opened the door. A glare was the only greeting I had for him.

He shuffled his feet and looked somber. "Look. I'm sorry. I owe you an apology."

"Fine," I said. "Apology accepted." I started to close the door.

He put his hand out, an unmistakable plea in his gray eyes. "Wait. Can we talk?"

I didn't want him in my house. I didn't want to listen to anything he had to say. "Why? Why should we talk? You obviously don't believe anything I have to say."

"That's not true. You caught me off guard. It just seemed so preposterous what you were telling me that—"

"Well, my story hasn't changed. It's still preposterous, so let's agree on that and let it go. Now, if you don't mind . . ." I expected him to step back from the door so I could close it, but instead he stepped forward, his hand still on the door.

"I was wrong. I'm sorry. Please. Can I come in?"

"How did you know where I live?" I asked, fixing him with a hard glare.

"I'm a cop. Besides, I knew you lived in Kate's house."

I heard the sound of TJ's feet coming down the stairs and a moment later he appeared at my side, looking at the stranger at the door. "Who's this?"

"I'm a friend of your mom's," Rob said. "You must be TJ." He extended his hand.

"Cool," TJ said, accepting the handshake.

I gave an exasperated sigh. "TJ, this is Rob Porter. He was just leaving."

Rob's eyes reflected his disappointment. "Yeah. Good to meet you, bud." He glanced at me in frustration. "Okay. Sorry to bother you."

"Mom, he doesn't have to leave just because I'm here. You can have friends over. You never have friends over."

I felt my cheeks redden. I closed my eyes for a moment to regroup, and breathed out. "Fine," I said through gritted teeth. "Rob, would you like to come in?"

He flashed a half smile and stepped around me. I closed the door and indicated the living room. When he was seated on the couch, I asked, "Can I get you anything?"

"What are you having?"

I picked up my glass of wine to carry to the kitchen. I would need a refill for this. "I have white wine. Is that okay?"

"That would be nice."

When I came back with the glasses of chardonnay, Rob and TJ were deep in conversation.

"Mom, he's a detective!" TJ said, a wide smile on his face.

"I know, sweetie."

"Are you here because of our ghosts?" he asked Rob.

Rob looked at me to gauge my reaction. When I said nothing, he said, "You have more than one?"

"I'm not sure. The first one said her name was Emma, but then she said there was a Marilee with her."

"Were you scared?"

"Oh, no. Mom was, though."

I rolled my eyes.

TJ regaled Rob with his experiences with the ghost, which I tolerated for a short while. My insides were churning and I had to work at keeping a smile on my face. For TJ's benefit.

After fifteen minutes, I told TJ it was time for bed. "Should I—"

"You can sleep in my room if you want," I said.

"Oh, Mom. I'm not scared of any ghosts."

"I didn't say you were. I might be, though."

"Okay, I can sleep in your room if you want me to." I could tell he didn't want Rob to think he was afraid, and I'd given him an out. His relief was palpable. He stuck his hand out to Rob. "Glad to meet you."

"Me, too, buddy."

Finally, Rob and I were alone. Emotions were tumbling over themselves in my head. Hurt was probably the most prevalent, slightly overshadowing anger and disappointment. I picked up my wine and took a sip, and then a bigger one, and stared at the glass.

"Kelly." He said it softly, as if trying to penetrate the fog of anger I'm sure he suspected cloaked me.

"You could run a background check on me, you know. See if I—"

"Stop it." He set his glass down on the coffee table, probably harder than he'd intended. I was surprised it didn't break. "I've said I'm sorry. I meant it. I was out of line. Can we put it behind us or do you plan to hold a grudge forever?"

"I'm sorry if I don't just bounce back after my integrity is questioned."

"And I wouldn't expect you to. You're right. Maybe it's too much to forgive." He stood. "Do you want me to go?"

"Yes." I hesitated. "No." He stood looking at me. "No," I said again.

He sat down on the couch next to me, his arms resting on his knees, head down. "So," he said, "what now?"

"As you can see, I'm not the only one who heard the ghost."

"You have a brave boy there."

"I do. But he shouldn't have to be."

"The thing about Marilee threw me off and I over-reacted. We're working hard to find her and I just didn't expect you to say what you did. I mean, it seemed so impossible that a ghost would . . . would . . . mention Marilee." He spread his hands helplessly, trying to convey to me the reason for his reaction.

I studied him for a moment, and felt my anger lessen. "I guess I understand. Maybe I overreacted, too. But you have to admit . . . Never mind. I accept your apology." I picked up my wineglass, and set it down again. "Do you think the fact that the ghost mentioned her means Marilee is dead?"

"God, I hope not. But it's a sobering thought."

"Do you know who Emma might be?"

He didn't answer right away. He scratched his head, and ran his fingers through his hair. "No, but I can check whether any other children are missing. The fact that I'm not aware of any could mean that it's been several years since something like that happened."

"Do you want to see TJ's room, see if anything jumps out at you?" I laughed softly. "I don't mean that in the literal sense."

He gave a crooked smile. "Okay." He took a gulp of his wine and left the glass on the coffee table.

"Of course, probably nothing will happen," I said as I led him up the stairs.

"Probably, but it can't hurt to check things out."

I stuck my head in TJ's room. As I'd hoped, he'd chosen to sleep in my room. "Here you go," I said, stepping aside to let Rob enter.

He glanced around the room, his eyes finally settling on the Dot. "Is that the famous Alexa?" he asked, noting the blue light that indicated Alexa was listening.

"Yes." I sat down on TJ's bed. Rob sat beside me, watching to see if I had a problem with that.

I looked at him, finger to my lips, and asked Alexa, "Is anyone here?"

No answer. I tried again after a moment. "Emma? Are you here?"

We sat silently for several minutes but there was no response from the Dot.

"Alexa, is anyone with you?"

Hmm. I don't know that one, said the voice.

"Does that sound like what you heard last night?"

"No. That's Alexa's normal speaking voice. I don't think Emma's here right now."

Rob picked up the unit and looked it over carefully, checking the cord plugged into the wall behind the dresser, and inspected the windows and floorboards. He turned to me and shrugged. "I don't see anything abnormal."

"I didn't either. I would've been surprised if you found anything. It's too weird to be just a frayed cord or open window. Sorry I can't show you what happened. It seems the ghosts are quiet tonight."

"When does the activity usually happen?"

"In the middle of the night. Probably after three."

"Then we're just too early. Do you want me to stick around? I could—"

"I don't think that would be a good idea. Besides, it doesn't happen every night so it might be a waste of your time."

"Okay. I just thought . . . I mean, I guess I should let you get back to doing whatever you were doing before I showed up. Sorry to drop in on you."

"Yeah, it's been a difficult day."

He followed me back down the stairs. "Let me know if anything happens tonight?"

"Sure. I'll see you later." I walked him to the door and closed it behind him.

Then I sank down on the couch and picked up my half-empty wine glass. He came to my house. Even though I had been angry, it felt good to have someone care enough to make an effort to apologize, especially knowing how upset I was. An inkling of guilt tried to weasel its way into my brain, but I had the presence of mind to refuse to let it in. I have nothing to feel guilty about. Although, if I was being honest, he was starting to grow on me. And if I was being really honest, I'd felt an attraction to him the first time I met him.

I downed the rest of my chardonnay, rinsed out the glasses and put them in the dishwasher. Looking toward the stairs, I wondered whether I should spend the night in TJ's room. Maybe I'd had just enough wine to do it.

I checked on TJ, who was sound asleep in my room, and took my things into the bathroom to get ready for bed, then stood at the door of TJ's room. I took a deep breath and stepped inside. Nothing was out of place and there was no sound coming from Alexa. I sat on the edge of the bed. "Hello?" I stared at the Dot, willing it to answer. Of course, it didn't. "Emma?" After five minutes, I turned off the lamp and climbed under the covers, leaving the bedroom door standing open, just in case.

Sunshine woke me up. I stretched languorously, my eyes flying open as I remembered where I was. I sat up and slid my feet to the floor. Everything was normal. I was both relieved and disappointed. Now I had no reason to contact Rob.

CHAPTER 18

It turned out that I didn't need a reason. He called me.

"I did some digging when I got to work this morning," he said. "I did find an Emma. Emma Corning went missing eight years ago. She was five years old. Her body was never found."

"Really? Poor little girl." I let out a breath. "But, is it even possible, you know, that she's talking through my Alexa? This freaks me out."

"It kinda freaks me out, too."

"What do we do about it?"

"We can hope she's still connected to the Alexa. We need to see if she can help us find her."

"So, you want me to sleep in TJ's room every night?"

"I hadn't got that far, but that's not a bad idea," he said. "Unless . . . you want me to."

"You can't spend the night in my house. It wouldn't be right. To quote you, I hardly know you."

"Can you please forget I said that?"

"Well, you did apologize. I guess I might be able to let it go.

"Could you? That would be great." He was silent for a moment. "What about, maybe we could set up a nanny cam in TJ's room."

"Do you think that would work?"

"I don't know, but it might be worth a try."

"Let's do it then."

"I'll pick something up and bring it over tonight. If that's okay with you."

"Sure." A thought popped into my mind and I blurted it out before I could stop myself. "You should plan to stay for dinner."

I could almost hear him smile through the phone.

"That would be great. I'll come over around six. Is that okay?"

"Can you make it five? I don't want it to be a late night for TJ."

"Sure."

"Great. I look forward to seeing you."

Hanging up, I felt a warm flush at the audacity of my actions. At least, it was audacious to me. I looked toward the ceiling. "Is it okay with you, Tom?" The twinge of guilt I hadn't allowed last night slithered around the edges of my mind. *I know it's okay with Tom. He'd want me to be happy.* Of course, then I had to chastise myself that I was jumping the gun. It was only dinner.

But I couldn't help feeling nervous that dinner might not be perfect.

CHAPTER 19

Rob seemed like a steak guy, and I could make a great steak. I did the shopping and most of the prep before I picked TJ up from the Methodist parking lot.

"Really, Mom?" TJ's eyes lit up when I told him Rob was coming to dinner.

"You don't mind?"

"No, Mom. He's so cool. Maybe tonight Emma will talk to him."

I might think Rob was cool, too.

The old house had a brick patio in the back with a grill. I hadn't used it yet but I'd dumped out the charcoal residue and scrubbed the grill. I found a bag of briquettes in the garage. The steaks were seasoned and sitting on the kitchen counter, corn on the cob was boiling on the stove and I was just starting to toss a Caesar salad when Rob arrived, right on time.

TJ greeted him with a big grin and led him into the kitchen. I offered him a beer and told him to relax while I finished. He offered to grill the steaks for me, but I told him I had it covered.

"Steak is one of my specialties," I said. "But you could finish tossing the salad for me if you wanted to."

"Sure," he said with a smile, and rubbed his hands together. "Whatever you need."

I had TJ set the table on the screened-in porch.

From the patio, I could hear him chattering to Rob. Rob had explained about the nanny cam and TJ was excited. He insisted he wanted to sleep in his own room so he wouldn't miss anything. He had many questions about what would happen if anything happened. I did, too.

Rob lavished compliments on me for grilling the steaks to perfection.

TJ piped up with, "My mom cooks everything great!"

A warm flush of embarrassment crept up my cheeks. I protested, but was pleased, and secretly pleased that Rob liked my dinner.

As we sat around the table on the porch, it almost felt like a family. And that scared me. I couldn't afford feelings like that. I'd lost too much. I didn't want something else to lose. Me and TJ. That was all I needed.

The fear that had flared in my brain slipped away as I settled into the conversation and sipped a beer. And watched TJ's full-on hero-worship. I couldn't decide whether or not it was a good thing to let TJ grow attached. The what-ifs stoked my fear again as I watched the interplay between the two of them, wondering what it would do to TJ if Rob... didn't stick around.

"Kelly?" Rob's voice brought me back to the real world. "Are you okay?"

I managed a small laugh. "Sure. Why?"

"You looked so deep in thought."

"I guess I was. Sorry." I quickly took a gulp of my beer. I pasted on a smile and said, "Anybody want dessert?" Without waiting for an answer, I picked up my empty plate and stacked TJ's and Rob's on top, then carried them to the kitchen. I dished up three bowls of vanilla ice cream and drizzled chocolate sauce on top, spritzed on whipped cream, set them on a tray and carried it out to the porch.

"Greatest dinner ever!" TJ said enthusiastically.

I shook my head, a wry smile on my face. *You can't protect him from everything.*

After the ice cream bowls were rinsed and added to the dishwasher, I found Rob and TJ huddled over a shopping bag. I arrived in time to see Rob pull a medium-sized teddy bear out of the bag.

"It was between a bear and a clown," he said. "And clowns are scary, aren't they?"

"They sure are," TJ responded. "I like the bear."

"Then let's go set it up."

TJ took the stairs two at a time while Rob and I followed at a more leisurely pace. Rob set the bear on the bedside table, its lens directed at the Alexa. He ushered us out of the room and back downstairs.

"May I?" he asked me, indicating my phone. I handed it

to him and he downloaded the app for the camera on my phone. "I could put it on my phone, too, if you want?"

That gave me pause, but it made sense. "Sure. Go ahead. Now we just have to wait."

Rob looked at TJ. "If the ghost should show up, be sure not to let it know there's a camera. It should be a secret. Because, if it turns out there isn't really a ghost, we don't want to tip anyone off that we're collecting evidence."

"Don't worry. I won't tell *anyone*." I could tell TJ was excited to be in on the potential sting operation. "Mom doesn't want me to tell anyone about our ghosts, either. I wish I could tell my friends."

Rob glanced at me. "I think your mom's right. Are you okay with keeping that secret, too?"

TJ shrugged. "I guess."

Rob squeezed his shoulder and smiled at him. "It'll be our secret then, just between the three of us."

"Cool," TJ said, his eyes bright at the thought of being part of a conspiracy with Rob.

"It's time for you to go get ready for bed, sweetie," I said. "You can sleep in my room if you want."

"*Mom*," he said in exasperation, as if the concept was over my head. "If I sleep in your room there won't be anyone for the ghost to talk to. I *have* to be in my room."

I shrugged. "Okay, then. Go for it."

"Can I come down to say goodnight to Rob?"

I ruffled his hair. "Of course you can."

Once he'd come down and said his goodnights, I was left alone with Rob. "Can I get you another beer?"

"Sure," he said, and followed me into the kitchen.

He leaned against the counter, sipping his beer and watching me. *Now what? Why had I offered him another beer?*

I cleared my throat. "I don't want to keep you. It was great of you to install the camera in TJ's room, but you don't have to hang around."

"Do you want me to go?"

I didn't answer.

"What were you thinking about earlier, during dinner?" he asked tentatively, maybe concerned that he was invading my privacy. "I mean, if you don't mind my asking. It just seemed . . . heavy, I guess."

I glanced at him, his gaze steady on mine. I hesitated, and cleared my throat again. "To be honest, the sight of you and TJ bonding . . . it scared me."

He looked confused.

"Sorry for being blunt, but TJ's been through enough . . . loss . . . in his life. I don't want to risk him getting hurt like that again."

"Have I done something—"

"No, it's not something you did. It's me, working through the complex issues that you have to work through when your husband dies." He didn't respond and, after a moment, I said, "I'm trying to manage my concerns, my fears. I apologize if I'm giving mixed signals."

"No apology necessary. Do you want me to—"

"No. If you mean do I want you to back off. I don't know what I want, but it's good for TJ to have a man to look up to. Just so long as you understand that I'm not looking for anything from you. I'm not ready for . . . whatever."

"Duly noted." He sipped his beer. "We can be friends, though, can't we?"

"Of course. I consider you a friend. I want you for a friend."

"Good, because otherwise it would be awkward if I rushed over in the middle of the night because your Alexa mouthed off."

I laughed, the tension easing. "Let's go sit down."

The beer tasted good. Normally, I'm a wino, in only the best sense of the word, but I could appreciate a cold beer under the right circumstances. I settled back in the couch and sipped my beer, wondering what my intentions were. I glanced at Rob, letting my gaze linger until he noticed. Caught, I took a gulp too fast and choked on it. My embarrassment had to be written all over my face, but he pretended not to notice. Score a point for him.

"So," I said.

"So," he replied. Waiting for me to signal the direction to take.

"I guess I—"

"It's getting late—"

We both spoke at once, and I said, "Sorry. You were saying?"

"Just, if you want me to go is all. I know it's probably late for you."

"Kind of. Besides, you might have to get up in the middle of the night, so you should probably try to get to bed early."

He laughed. "This should be interesting." He set his empty bottle on the coffee table and stood. "Thanks for dinner. It was great."

"You helped make it that way."

"No, you did all the hard stuff," he protested with a smile. "I had fun tonight."

"Me, too. We'll have to do it again sometime."

"That would be nice."

I walked him to the front door. He turned to face me and paused, and I wondered if he meant to kiss me, but he dipped his head and said "Good night," and was gone.

And I was left with a stomach full of butterflies and heart full of confused disappointment.

CHAPTER 20

Rob texted first thing the next morning to see if I'd noticed anything. I hadn't, but we couldn't rule out that maybe whatever activity had occurred hadn't awakened TJ, so Rob offered to stop by after work to go over the video with me. Since I wasn't confident that I understood how the nanny cam worked, it made sense for him to come show me how to do it. At least, that's what I told myself.

I texted that he should come over and I would order a pizza. I didn't want to give him the idea that dinner together was going to be a regular thing, but if he was going to go out of his way for us, it was only fair for me to feed him. Pizza was a good compromise. Uncluttered.

I felt lighthearted, and energetic. After getting home from dropping TJ off at camp, I put on a pair of shorts and tank top and laced up my running shoes and headed out the backdoor for a run. I ran for an hour, juggling thoughts ranging from grief to anticipation. I briefly flirted with the idea of a me-and-Rob, but topped that thought with a resolve to maintain an appropriate distance from him. Because ... it was just too soon.

Later, after picking TJ up, we stopped at Molly's and picked up a chocolate cream pie for dessert. In spite of vowing that this was only going to be a casual get-together to go over the camera footage, I couldn't help the urge to do something special.

"HE'S HERE," TJ CALLED FROM THE living room. I came out from the kitchen in time to see my son open the door and the affectionate way Rob ruffled his hair. To be honest, my heart skipped a beat.

"Beer or wine?" I asked as Rob and TJ plopped down on the couch. "Beer for me, Mom," TJ said with what I'm sure he thought was a wicked grin, and I responded with a motherly frown.

"I'll second that," Rob said.

"Aw, Mom," TJ said when he saw the glass of milk I brought out for him. "Why can't I have something good to drink like you guys?"

"Your other choice is flavored water. Does that sound better?"

"Yes, it does," he said, putting up his hand to block any attempt I might make to hand him the milk. "I want the orange one."

I set the beer in front of Rob. "I'll be right back. His highness isn't happy."

Walking away, I heard TJ say, "Should I go get the nanny cam?"

"No need. The video streams on my phone. We'll look at it when your mom comes back."

I carried my beer into the living room, but before I could sit down the doorbell rang. "That will be the pizza," I said, reaching in my pocket for the twenty I'd slipped in. Rob started to stand, but I said, "I'll get it."

"Eat first or watch video first?" Rob asked.

"The pizza's hot. I think we should take advantage and eat it now."

Rob followed me into the kitchen and I handed him paper plates and napkins. His hand brushed mine, and I involuntarily said "Oh" and pulled my hand away.

"I'm sorry," he said, clearly befuddled.

"It's okay," I said quickly. "It just startled me." I was immediately embarrassed by my overreaction.

He pretended nothing had happened, which made me more ashamed. What did I think I was, a prize men were drooling over? I seemed to take every opportunity to view Rob's simplest actions through the lens of his trying to hit on me. He'd always been a perfect gentleman around me, apologizing for things he didn't even do. Poor guy. What must he think of me?

TJ was bouncing up and down on the couch, impatient that it was taking so long to watch the footage from the nanny cam. I told him we'd watch while we ate pizza and served up a piece to each of us.

Rob gobbled his first piece of pizza, then wiped his hands on a napkin and started the video. "There may not be anything to see," he said. "TJ, you didn't wake up during the night and didn't remember hearing the voices, so it's possible last night was a dud. Let's watch and see."

He turned out to be right. He fast-forwarded the video, stopping at intervals to listen, but there was nothing.

TJ was disappointed, and kept an eye on the real-time video while we finished eating. I carried the paper plates and pizza box into the kitchen, asking over my shoulder whether Rob wanted another beer.

"I'll get us both one," he said, following me into the kitchen.

I pulled the chocolate cream pie out of the refrigerator and he smiled in anticipation. I showed him where to find the dessert plates while I cut slices for each of us.

"Mom!"

"I'll be there in a minute," I called out.

"You have to come now, Mom!"

Rob and I exchanged glances and headed back to the living room.

"Look," TJ said, pointing at the screen.

Before we had a chance to see what TJ was looking at, we heard the sound of crying.

"What the—" Rob said, taking the phone from TJ.

I leaned over his shoulder to see, a shiver running down my back. The bedroom curtains were fluttering, even though the window was closed.

"Maybe we can get it to talk to us," TJ said, "Let's go see." The three of us dashed for the stairs.

Outside the bedroom door, I held a finger to my lips. "We don't want to scare it away."

"*We* don't want to scare a ghost," Rob said with a wry grin. "Okay. Got it."

Rob stared in awe at the Dot, as the sobbing grew in volume. When we were all in the room, the door slammed shut of its own volition behind us.

"Mom?" TJ said, his eyes big.

"It's okay, sweetie," I said, pulling him into a hug.

I breathed deeply. "Are you there?" Nothing but sobbing. "Emma? Is that you?"

The sudden chill had us peering around the room. Whatever breeze had ruffled the curtains in the video picked up speed, and my hair flew around my face.

"Emma. Talk to us." I had to raise my voice over the sound of the wind.

The sobbing stopped and an eerie *Help us* emanated from the Dot.

"Emma? We want to help you, but we don't know how. Talk to us."

Help us, the child's voice said.

"Where are you? Can you tell us so we can find you?"

Nothing answered for such a long time I thought it must have gone. Then, *I don't know.*

"Emma, there are three of us here who want to help you.

I'm Kelly, TJ is my son and Rob is our friend. Will you talk to us?"

The wind howled up to and through the ceiling and the door flew open. The cold seeped from the room and all was quiet. We sat on TJ's bed for twenty minutes, but there was no more activity. Disappointed, we trudged back to the living room.

"Oh. The pie," I said, suddenly remembering that I'd left it sitting out on the kitchen counter.

"It'll still taste good," Rob said. "No matter what condition it's in."

"Thanks, you optimist," I said with a laugh. "I'll check on it."

The pie was a little soft and droopy, but I doubted that would put any of us off, so I carried the plates to the living room and handed them out.

I took a bite and savored the creamy chocolate and whipped cream, then fixed a glare on Rob. "So, what do you think now?"

He swallowed the bite he'd just put in his mouth. "I don't know what the hell to think. I've never seen anything like it."

"It wasn't scary when you were there," TJ said.

"You weren't scared?" Rob asked with a grin. "Because I sure was."

"Nope. I thought it was cool." TJ's smile filled his whole face.

Rob looked at me. "Well, I don't know about you, but that really freaked me out. You seem to be okay with it."

"Don't forget, I've been through this a few times. And, to be honest, it was a lot less scary because you were there." I nodded toward TJ, who was engrossed in watching the nanny cam footage on Rob's phone. "And I'm pretty sure the same can be said for him."

I took another bite, taking a moment to appreciate the rich, smooth chocolate. "We have to figure out what to do next. It seems to want to talk to us."

Rob raked his fingers through his hair but didn't say anything right away. Finally, he said, "We need to ask questions. It seemed impossible before that any of it was real, but now I've seen it for myself. And, implausible or not, Emma might know something about Marilee."

"Yeah, she might. Now what?"

"So now . . . how do you feel about a slumber party?"

CHAPTER 21

"A what?" His suggestion took me by surprise. My brain swirled with all the implications.

"It might be important to be vigilant. What if Emma comes back? We should be there to question her. With Marilee's life on the line, I think we should try." He looked embarrassed. "I know this is probably uncomfortable for you, so, if it makes you feel better, I can just wait for you to call me."

"It's not that. Well, okay, maybe it *is* that, but I suppose you're right." I smiled. "Should you deputize me or something?"

"Funny."

"We could pull a couple of chairs in there. It will be a long night and the more comfortable we can be the better."

Rob followed me out of the kitchen. TJ was still holding Rob's phone, but his attention had switched over to the Disney Channel. He glanced up when we approached.

He held out the phone to Rob. "Nothing happened." There was no mistaking the disappointment on his face.

"Too bad, sweetie," I said. "If it makes you feel any better, we're all going to sleep in your room tonight in case Emma comes back."

"You mean Rob, too?"

"Yes. It was Rob's idea to have a slumber party."

"What's a slumber party?"

"It's usually a few teenage girls spending the night together, watching videos and making fudge and talking about boys."

TJ looked at me with a look questioning why anyone would think that was fun.

"We won't be talking about boys at our slumber party," I said.

"Can we still make fudge?"

"Yeah, can we?" Rob piped in.

"Maybe not fudge," I said. "I do, however, have brownie mix. Will that do?"

"Yeah!" TJ said.

I smacked my forehead with the heel of my palm. "I don't know why I suggested that. We just had chocolate cream pie not even an hour ago."

Rob grinned. "Special circumstances," he said and winked at me.

"Okay, but not for at least an hour. Your teeth are going to fall out from all that chocolate."

TJ rubbed his hands together gleefully. "It will be worth it."

I pulled him in for a hug. "You guys go scout around to find comfortable chairs to sit in while we stay up all night, okay?"

TJ shot up. "I know just the chair." He turned to Rob. "Mom has this cool chair in her room. It rocks. I have a rocking chair in my room but it's all wood and not comfortable like Mom's. Hers has cushions. It's kinda big. Can you help me move it?"

"Sure. Lead the way."

I insisted Rob use the chair from my room. Despite his protests, I'd take the wooden rocker. I wanted him to be comfortable, since he was sacrificing his entire night for us. Blankets and pillows would make the wooden rocker fine for me, and TJ could have his bed. I expected he'd be nodding off before too long anyway.

I followed the boys into my room. Rob couldn't miss the picture of me and Tom, arms around each other, which was prominently displayed. He glanced at me for a moment.

"That's my dad," TJ said.

"I thought it must be," Rob said solemnly, and gently ruffled TJ's hair before making a beeline for the chair in the corner.

I WAS RUNNING THROUGH A FOREST. Someone was crying and I needed to find them. Wet branches slapped me in the face and I vaulted over fallen logs until I tripped and had to crawl on my hands and knees. The crying was so close, morphing into to a plea: *Help meeee.* "I'm coming," I said, struggling to get the words out, each seeming cast in sludge.

The sudden icy temperature snapped me out of my dream. Sobs came from Alexa, and I saw Rob jump to his feet.

"It's starting," he said.

"I dozed off. I'm sorry," I said.

"It's 3 a.m. You get a pass. It's freezing in here."

Cold settled on the room like a blanket of ice, and TJ bolted upright. "Mom?"

"It's okay, sweetie. We're here. I think Emma's here, too."

I approached the Dot, and sat on the end of TJ's bed. I glanced at Rob and TJ, and said, "Emma, we're here to help you. Can you talk to us?"

The wait seemed interminable. "Mom, when's she going to answer?"

"I hope soon."

If it hadn't been that the room was still freezing, I might have thought we were out of luck. I hugged my arms around my body to warm up.

The sobbing started again.

"Emma, please talk to us. We can't help you if we don't know where you are or what you're dealing with." I glanced at Rob. "You can trust us."

It's scary here.

Rob sat beside me on the end of the bed and put his hand over mine. I felt a tingle, but now wasn't the time to dwell on his touch.

"Emma, it's Rob. I'm a policeman and I really want to find you. Can you tell us where you are?"

I don't know.

He squared his shoulders. "Is anyone with you, Emma?"

Yes.

It seemed for a moment she wouldn't say more, but then she said the name we dreaded hearing, *Marilee.*

I could see by the stark expression on his face that he was afraid of what that meant.

"Emma, is Marilee . . . still alive?" I asked.

She is.

I closed my eyes for a fraction of a second to gather courage for my next question, barely able to get the words out. "Are you?"

There was no answer right away. Maybe the question put her off.

I looked at Rob, then back at the Dot.

No.

I squeezed his hand, my heart clenching for the poor dead child.

"Oh, Emma." I couldn't keep the sadness out of my voice. "You need to help us find you. Can you help us?"

I'll try.

"Maybe it will help if you can describe where you are, what you see around you."

It's dark. I can't see.

"Where's Marilee," Rob asked.

She's here but she's sleeping. That's all she can do. I don't think it will take long.

"What won't take long?" Rob's voice reflected his anxiety.

I think Marilee will be dead soon.

"Why do you think that, Emma?"

He stopped coming here and she's so hungry. I think he means for her to be hungry until it's over.

"Emma, please," I said. "There must be something you can tell us about where you are. Are you outside, or in a house?"

The bars keep her in.

Tears streamed down my cheeks, and I used the hand not held by Rob to brush them away.

"You can get out of the bars, can't you?"

I can go in and out, but I don't want to leave my friend.

"She's lucky to have you there. She must be so afraid."

I glanced to Rob for help.

"Emma, can you go outside and see what's around the house, or the . . . cage . . . or whatever is holding you and Marilee? If you can give us a clue, we might be able to figure out where to look."

I remember what it felt like when there wasn't food anymore. I didn't like it.

"Oh, my God," I said, unable to stop the flow of tears. Rob let go of my hand and pulled me to him, his arm holding me against his chest.

I buried my face in his shoulder. "What kind of monster could do that to a child?"

He smoothed my hair and gave me a moment to pull myself together. I sniffed and sat up again.

"Who did this to you, Emma?"

A man. He brought Marilee.

"The same man took you both?" Rob asked.

He looked the same but old.

"Can you tell us where we should look for you, Emma?" I asked.

"Is it a neighborhood, in the woods, something like that?" Rob added.

There's trees. And water.

"It sounds like the woods. Does that sound right?" Rob asked.

The trees are crying.

"Crying? What do you mean?"

I have to go now.

The room warmed up quickly, and I knew she was gone. The three of us exchanged glances. It had been an unbelievable experience.

"Mom," TJ said, tears clinging to his eyelashes, "I'm so scared for her."

"Me, too, honey." I pulled away from the safety of Rob's arms and stood.

"I need coffee," I said. "Anyone want to join me?"

"I get coffee?" TJ asked, his eyes wide.

"No, honey, but you can have hot chocolate. Will that be okay?"

"Sure." He clambered out of bed and followed me out the door, Rob bringing up the rear.

I started the coffee brewing and heated milk in a saucepan for the chocolate. Rob seemed to catch the drift that we'd talk about Emma after we were settled at the table with our beverages.

I poured the milk in a mug and stirred in some Hershey's cocoa and slid the mug to TJ.

"Can I have whipped cream on it?" he asked, sliding it back.

I found the can of whipped cream in the refrigerator and squirted it on the steaming hot chocolate and slid it back to him. Given that it was still the middle of the night, I wasn't surprised to see TJ rubbing his eyes. When he noticed me watching, he flashed a tired grin. I put a gentle hand on his shoulder and smiled back.

"Okay now?"

"Just the way I like it," he said, grinning.

I filled two more mugs with coffee and set them, along with half 'n' half and sugar, on the table. On a whim, I squirted whipped cream on top of my coffee.

No one knew quite what to say, so we concentrated on our drinks.

Rob finally piped up. "That was insane."

"I think I'd be freaking out if you weren't here. I'd have probably packed up TJ again and headed for the motel."

"I get it. I'd hate to experience that alone, too."

"Do you think it could really be happening? Did we imagine it?"

"Mom, it really happened. Emma's our ghost."

"Leave it to the child," I said, shooting TJ a smile. "I know, honey. Besides, we're experienced now. Were you scared?"

"Heck, no. Emma's just a kid, like me."

"Yes, she is." I reached over and patted his leg.

"What's going to happen to her?" he asked, his little forehead creased in worry.

"I hope we're going to be able to find her," I said.

"But, if we find her . . . what will we do then?"

"We'll tell the police."

"Like Rob?" TJ's worried glance turned to Rob.

"Like me," Rob said. "We just have to get there in time to save Marilee."

"But what about Emma?" TJ asked, not ready to let it go. "We have to save her."

I sighed and put my hand over his. "We want to save both of them." Wearily, I turned to my cup of coffee and took a couple of sips before setting it down again.

"Finish your hot chocolate so you can get some rest," I said to TJ. "You can sleep in my room."

"Aw, Mom." TJ glared at me then attempted to down his remaining hot chocolate in one gulp, and ended up with his face and pajamas drenched in chocolate. "Oops."

"Oops is right." I shook my head as I grabbed a kitchen towel and mopped at his wet face and pajamas. I gently swatted him on the butt. "Go on upstairs and wash your face and put on clean pajamas. I'll be up in a little while. Mr. Porter and I need to talk."

"Okay. I'm sorry, Mom."

"I know, honey. It's okay."

I watched him slink off toward the stairs, head hanging, then turned to Rob. "Where were we?"

"I think we need to go back over what she told us. If she's right, Marilee might not have much time left."

"I know. I'm horrified by that. You're much more familiar with this area than I am. Did anything she said stick out?"

"Not really. Woods and water are everywhere around here. The town backs up to a forest; there are miles of woodland. And more than one body of water."

"What do you think she meant about crying trees?" I asked.

"Weeping willows, maybe? That's all I can think of"

"She said bars, Rob. Like Marilee's in a cage. It's too awful to think about." My eyes started to fill and he reached over and squeezed my hand.

"It's not good. But it makes sense. I've read about cases where abducted kids were kept in all kinds of terrible conditions. Closets, trunks, sheds. The stuff of nightmares. The ones found alive . . . well, let's just say it really messes them up."

"My heart hurts. Knowing there are monsters out there who prey on children. If something happened to TJ, I don't know if I could survive."

His face was grim, his mouth set in a tight line. "Yeah," was all he said.

"Should we search the woods tomorrow?"

"Too many miles of woods and shoreline."

"But at least it's something. Do you remember seeing any bodies of water with weeping willows growing on the banks?"

"I can think of a few places I could check out."

"I'll come with you," I said.

"Absolutely not. If we're dealing with a predator, I don't want you anywhere near him."

"But I—"

"It's a police matter. You don't have the training or experience to deal with a dangerous situation."

"It may be a police matter, but you only have this lead because of me. Or, because of my Alexa. If you don't want to take me with you, I'll see if Jen wants to go hiking."

"That's a bad idea."

"Look, whoever he is, he has no idea we're on to him. People probably hike around those woods all the time. There's no reason for him to think we're a threat."

"I think you should let the police investigate."

"Are you going to tell them a ghost told you to look for weeping willows?"

"Obviously not." He blew out a breath and ran his hand through his hair.

I grabbed my phone off the coffee table. "I'm going to text Jen and see if she has plans for today. It would help if you gave me an idea of the areas with the weeping willows."

"It would help if I went with you. You don't have to ask Jen."

"So, what time do we leave?"

CHAPTER 22

When it was a decent hour to phone without worrying about waking her up, I called Kevin's mom, Melissa, to see if she'd mind watching TJ for a few hours. She came through for me. She said I could drop TJ off around nine, assuring me Kevin was going to be thrilled.

I met Rob at the Old Miner trailhead, where he was waiting for me, leaning against his truck. He looked... appropriate. Okay, he looked good. A loose-fitting tank top exposed his muscular arms, and dark jeans and hiking boots completed his attire. I caught myself staring and coughed to cover my embarrassment. I'd been prescient enough to wear jeans and boots myself, in spite of the heat and humidity I was sure the day would bring, and the red tank I wore ensured he wouldn't lose me.

"Where to, pardner?" I asked in my best faux western accent.

"We're going to follow that trail for a bit. I'm glad you wore protective clothing, as parts of the trail are rough, a lot of rocks and underbrush once we leave the trail. Some of the areas I'm thinking of line the banks of Bluebird Lake. That's where some of the weeping willows grow down to the edge of the water." He shifted his backpack up on his shoulders. "Did you bring water?"

"Yeah. I have a couple in my backpack."

"Me, too. I guess we're ready to go." He started up the trail and I hurried to catch up.

We stuck to the trail for twenty minutes. The beech and oaks lent a serenity to the woods that felt incongruous with our reason for being there. The pines towering overhead provided sparse shade, not enough to make a difference in the humid heat. We veered off the trail and crossed a footbridge over a swiftly flowing creek. Rob offered his hand to help steady me on the bridge. My breath caught, but I shrugged off the feeling of my hand in his. Now wasn't the time.

The overgrown footpath angled down, and the gurgling sound of water ahead of us was growing louder. Embedded rocks littering the path made walking tricky. My foot slipped off one of them and I was afraid I'd twisted it, but I was lucky and other than a twinge didn't have trouble walking. Tomorrow might be a different story.

"You okay?" Rob asked coming back to where I was testing my ankle. "Want to rest awhile?"

"I'm okay. I can walk and I'm not tired yet, so let's keep going."

"If you're sure," he said, watching me for a minute before turning back to the path.

My first few steps felt a little off but, after those, I had no further problem.

We broke through the trees, and the lake spread out in front of us. For a moment, I savored the fragrance of the dense foliage. If color had a smell, then I smelled green.

There was a short drop from the forest edge to the shoreline, which I tried to navigate on my own. When my feet slid out from under me on the loose limestone I let out a shriek. Rob, following behind, was close enough to catch me before I did any damage to myself, and I found myself gazing up into his eyes as he lifted me down to the shore.

I glanced away before it got awkward. For me. I don't think he thought anything about it. He asked if I was all right, then let me go.

Scanning the shoreline, Rob pointed to willows a dozen yards to the left. He offered me his hand, but I declined and followed him as we picked our way along the rocky shore. I watched him, his steps sure, probably from a lifetime spent around these woods and lakes, as I did my best not to trip or stumble.

Drawing near, I wondered what, exactly, we were looking for. The tips of willow branches trailed in the water and insects buzzed in the still air. I stepped into a cloud of gnats and frantically waved my arms and ducked below them as I rushed to Rob's side. His good-natured grin kind of pissed me off.

I narrowed my eyes at him in irritation, but my large dark glasses totally diffused the glare.

"How do we search around here?" I asked. "Do we crawl under the branches or what?" I didn't see anything that looked like a structure or hiding place, and wondered if it was my inexperience that kept me from noticing clues.

"A little of that. I've been scanning the banks and up into the tree line as we approached, but there's nothing. I'll check under the willow. You wait out here." His arm parted the willowy branches and he glanced over his shoulder at me. "Don't let the bugs get you." The branches closed behind him before I could sputter out a proper response. Then I laughed. *Oh, lighten up,* I admonished myself.

It didn't take long before he reemerged. "Nothing here. Let's move on."

Rob was up the bank in two steps, while I sort of clambered up, relying on my hands to help, not quite as sure-footed as my guide. On flatter ground, I wiped my hands together to dislodge the fine gravel imbedded in the heels of my hands, then tromped after him.

The heat was starting to get to me and, after navigating the rough footpaths for another half hour, I was ready to take a break. I pulled out a couple of water bottles and tossed one to Rob. He sat on a boulder watching me inspect my arms for bites and scratches. No doubt I'd look great tomorrow.

I sat next to him, wiping my sweaty forehead with the back of my hand. Rob pulled a bandana out of his backpack.

"It's an extra one. It really helps."

"Thanks," I said, wiping my face with it, then tucked it into my back pocket.

"Where to next?" I asked.

"Half a mile further we'll angle back down to the lake. By the way," he said, "you might want some of this." He handed me a bottle of bug spray.

"Oh, my God. Thanks! The mosquitos are getting relentless." I spritzed the solution on my arms and neck and patted some on my face.

"Sorry. I should have offered you some before we started out, but I sprayed it on before I left the house this morning and forgot."

"Oh, no problem. I'm okay. I should have done the same thing. Next time, I'll know."

Pushing up off the boulder, I blew out my cheeks and followed Rob's lead. I did my best to keep up, but had to admit I was starting to lag behind. I hadn't done much hiking in years, and the heat and humidity were taking a toll. Up ahead, Rob stopped and waited for me, extending a hand.

"Let me help you out there. This is grueling, especially on someone who's not used to it." He waited for me to accept his offer of help. "Come on. I won't bite."

Trying not to look too grateful, I grabbed his hand. It did make the trek easier to have someone pulling me along. I was very aware of our clasped hands for the first few minutes, then it felt natural. I didn't notice when that happened, but when Rob stopped and turned down a dirt path leading back toward the water, I stared at our hands in embarrassment and pulled mine away under the pretext of grabbing the bandana to wipe my face. I couldn't look at him for a few moments as my thoughts and emotions swirled. It would be so easy, with him. *But I'm not ready. I'm not, am I?*

I'm not. At least for now. Any thoughts I had about feelings I could have for Rob were covered over by the solemnity of our task.

This path was short and mostly flat all the way to the water. There were willows to both our left and the right. Rob parted the branches on the trees to the left and disappeared under them. I looked after him for a second, then slipped off my backpack, squared my shoulders and picked my way through the branches of the willow on the right. This close to the lake, the branches were dense and reached all the way to the ground. It was almost cave-like inside the branches, and peaceful. A breeze caused the limbs to dance, with a soft sigh of leaves brushing together. Children would love playing in the hollow formed by the trailing branches. As a child, I would have treasured this space. It could have been a secret clubhouse for me and my friends. As a parent, however, I would not have been comfortable for my child to play here, out of my sight and so close to the water.

It was cool and dark in the shadow of the tree, and I could hear the buzzing of insects. I found nothing under the tree but branches and dirt and water. I moved to the water's edge for a quick peek but, when I turned to go back, my foot slipped and I toppled into the lake, letting out a yell as water rose around my head. I sputtered, flailing and coughing as water filled my mouth.

"Hang on!" Rob was suddenly there, grabbing me under my arms and pulling me out of the water. "Are you okay?" He picked me up and carried me out from under the willow's swaying limbs.

He set me on a rock heated by the sun and brushed my wet hair out of my eyes, kneeling in front of me to inspect my face, then pulled off his tank and used it to wipe me down, all the time saying "I'm sorry."

Holding his wet tank top in one hand, he stood. "I should never have agreed to bring you along. I knew this was a bad idea."

I clambered to my soggy feet, hands on my hips. "Just because I wasn't careful enough doesn't mean you shouldn't have brought me."

"Yes it does. I should have realized—"

"There's nothing to realize. It was one damn slip. I'm fine. See." I glared and felt around the top of my head. "Hey, I think I lost my sunglasses." I turned and looked back at the path leading to the lake, and started back down.

Rob grabbed my arm. "You're not going back in there. The water's deep in some places and—"

"I want my glasses," I said, jerking my arm away.

Before I could take another step, he blocked my way. "I'll go look. You wait here."

He was gone before I could bite his head off. Why was I so mad? Embarrassment? Maybe I was mad at myself. Maybe next time, this little mishap would be all it took to convince him to leave me behind.

My drenched ponytail straggled down my back and I pulled out the band and shook my hair out. I fluffed it with my fingers, but it was hopeless.

I heard rustling and he came back through the branches, holding out my glasses. "They were on the bank, luckily."

I snatched them out of his hand and crammed them on my face. I turned to stomp off, but quickly turned back and threw my arms around his neck, shocking the hell out of him. And me, too.

"I'm sorry. You saved me and I yelled at you. I wasn't being careful enough, but I don't repeat mistakes. It won't happen again. I don't want you to leave me out of this."

He shook his head and stared into space in contemplation. I think he was mad, too.

I held my breath until he looked back at me. "I'm sorry," I said again in a small voice.

"No problem," he said stiffly. He slipped his wet tank back over his head. I watched, taken aback by the sight of his naked chest and shoulders. I'd been too angry to notice before, but now I sucked in a breath at his beautiful, muscular body.

He caught me looking and opened his mouth to say something, but then picked up my backpack. "We should head back."

I spread my arms. "No kidding. Look at me. I look like a drowned rat."

His eyes swept my body and I felt self-conscious, knowing my red tank top was plastered to my chest. I wrapped my arms around myself. "That's enough looking," I said, daring to smile.

His eyes moved up from my body to my eyes, and held there for a long moment. Then he nodded.

"Forgive me?" I asked, touching his arm.

He looked down at my hand then up to my face. "Nothing to forgive. You're not the first rookie I've had to pull out of a tough situation."

"I'm a rookie?"

"You're definitely a rookie. Now let's get you back." His face lightened up. "I could say let's get you out of those wet clothes, but I suppose that would be inappropriate."

I laughed. "Totally inappropriate." I slipped my arm through his and hugged it to my side. "I can carry my own backpack. You've been enough of a hero."

"You can never be enough of a hero. It's a full-time job."

I rolled my eyes.

My shoes squished as I walked. It was kind of a creepy feeling, warm and soggy. The heat of the day soon had my wet clothes feeling hot, although they were probably too soaked to dry out before we made it back to the car.

We walked in silence for a while until I asked, "What do we do next?"

"*We* don't do anything," he said, holding up a hand to silence my imminent protest. "We can't cover enough ground from land. I'll take out the department's boat to scan the shoreline."

"Are you taking me?"

"No."

"But—"

"I couldn't explain why you'd be there. There's paperwork to take out the boat and I'd have to include you in the paperwork. It would be frowned upon, believe me."

My shoulders slumped. "We have to work fast to find Marilee before she starves to death."

He stopped and looked at me, his eyes reflecting the seriousness of the situation. "I'm well aware of that. I'll take the boat out this afternoon."

We didn't talk much the rest of the way back. I wasn't sure what to say as we stood at our cars. Finally, I said something innocuous. "You'll let me know if you find anything?"

"Of course."

We shuffled our feet awkwardly, as if there were more to say. After a moment, I gave a small wave and headed for my car.

Once behind the wheel, I glanced toward Rob's car, and caught him watching me. I smiled and drove away.

CHAPTER 23

I stopped at home to change before picking up TJ. After a quick shower, I blew dry my hair and put on clean jeans and a T-shirt. I balled up my still-damp clothes to drop in the laundry room but, before I moved two feet, I heard a door slam. A chill ran up my spine. No one was in the house but me. I did a quick search for something to use as a weapon. Unfortunately for me, I didn't have an arsenal in my bedroom. A wooden coat hanger was the most deadly thing I could find. Sticking my head out of the room, holding the coat hanger protectively in front of me, I straightened when I saw TJ's bedroom door was closed. It hadn't been when I passed it half an hour ago.

I held my breath and turned the knob. As I expected, the room was empty. I had a feeling Emma wanted to talk. Considering whether I should text Rob, I decided against it. He would probably be on a boat continuing the search for Marilee.

"Emma?" I called, sitting on the end of TJ's bed. "Are you here? Do you want to talk?"

I'm here. Please hurry.

"We're trying, Emma. We looked along the banks of the lake this morning, but didn't find anything. Rob is taking out a boat to scour the shoreline this afternoon. Can't you tell us anything that could help us find you?"

The room grew colder and I wrapped my arms around myself to take the chill off. Emma didn't respond but after a moment I heard sobbing.

"Emma, don't give up. We're trying as hard as we can. Please, can't you look around, go outside, see if there's anything that might tell us where you are?"

There were so many letters. I see water out the window and a blue boat. I just see trees everywhere. Hurry.

The room warmed up and I knew she was gone.

I felt helpless. Water and a blue boat. How would that help? And what did she mean by letters? I texted Rob Emma's clues, then headed off to pick up TJ while I waited for Rob's answer.

When I got to Kevin's house, Melissa invited me in for coffee but I begged off, offering a brief recap of my grueling day, the lake part, that is, and pleaded a headache. My head really did hurt, but only because it was pulled in so many different directions.

I attempted to concentrate while TJ chattered about his adventures with Kevin. I smiled and tried to be an enthusiastic listener, but I kept going over in my head what Emma had told me, and worry over Marilee was ever-present.

Rob texted back asking if I wanted to stop by and fill him in on what Emma had said, saying it was okay to bring TJ with me. Not wanting to text and drive, I called him back.

"Uh oh." I could hear him cringe through the phone. "I can't remember what shape my condo's in."

"You're embarrassed for me to see where you live?"

"I'm not sure. It might be okay, but there might be dishes in the sink."

"Can't help you out there, buddy," I laughed. "I guess we'll have to wait and see. By the way, TJ's thrilled to go to your house."

"I'm not sure I can handle the pressure of possibly disappointing him."

"I'll try to manage his expectations before we get there."

I will admit to being curious to see Rob's home. I wondered if I would be put off if it was messy. Not that it should matter to me. I mean, we weren't dating or anything.

I needn't have worried. His condo was neat and nicely furnished with a comfortable seating area and bright kitchen. And no dishes in the sink.

"Looks like you didn't have to worry about what shape your house would be in." I rolled my eyes at him. "Mr. Clean."

"You say that like it's a bad thing," he said.

"Not at all. I'm impressed."

"I'm glad I could impress you. You can be a tough audience sometimes."

"What do you mean by that? I'm delightful."

"Delightfully stubborn maybe."

While Rob got us something to drink, I sank down on the sectional couch and motioned for TJ to join me. He was busy examining everything in the living room. There were a couple of citations on the wall and a trophy for a softball championship.

"Look, Mom. Rob was a Marine!" TJ said excitedly.

"Really?" I joined him at a bookcase where Rob's dog tags lay at the foot of a photograph of three Marines in a desolate-looking terrain. Probably Afghanistan. I hadn't known he was in the service, although I shouldn't have been surprised.

By this time, Rob was back in the room, carrying two coffee mugs, a bottle of water tucked under one arm.

"You were a Marine." TJ's smile almost took up his whole face.

Rob smiled back. "Ooh-rah!"

"What does that mean?" TJ looked perplexed.

"That's the way Marines talk," Rob said.

"Can I say it, too?"

"Sure, buddy. Ooh-Rah!"

"Ooh-Rah!" TJ proudly said back.

"Come on, you jarheads," I said.

"What—"

I held up my hand to ward off TJ's question. "It's a Marine thing. You wouldn't understand."

TJ looked at me with his mouth open, and Rob laughed and mouthed "Jarhead?"

I filled Rob in on what Emma had said about the letters, and my confusion over what she meant. If nothing else, it was an intriguing clue.

By now it was almost five and, being exhausted from our long day in the woods, I stood to go. As an afterthought, I asked Rob if he wanted to come over for a quick bite to eat.

"Sure."

"I can throw something together. It won't be anything fancy. We can figure it out after you get there."

Once home, TJ headed upstairs to put his backpack in his room, and I flopped down on the couch. What I wouldn't have given to climb into bed and shut my eyes for a couple of hours. It wouldn't be fair, though. I needed to spend time with TJ, and I'd invited Rob for dinner.

Almost before I had time to turn on the TV for TJ, there was a knock at the front door, and Rob stood on the porch with a pizza box in his hand. I gave a silent *Yay*. Pizza meant I didn't have to cook.

We sat at the kitchen table devouring the pizza. I contributed a couple of bottles of beer to the party. I could tell Rob was anxious to talk more about my session with Emma, but was hesitant to go into too much depth in front of TJ, who'd been excitedly telling us about the *Avengers* movie starting at seven. Perfect. At five to seven I told him he'd better hurry so he didn't miss the beginning. He excused himself and left Rob and me alone.

"Tell me again exactly what she said," Rob said. "In case you forgot something the first time."

I repeated our conversation verbatim. It had been short and sweet. When I was done, Rob looked as confused as I was.

"What do you think she means by 'letters?'" he asked.

"I don't know. Maybe ABC letters? Mail? Emma vanished before explaining what she meant. I'm not sure this helps us at all."

"We can't rule it out. Maybe she'll have more to say next time we talk to her."

"Something must have upset her, because she slammed TJ's door to get my attention. But she's so cryptic. What about you? Did you spot anything from the boat?"

"No. I pulled close to the shore wherever I saw stands of willows, but came up empty."

"She kept saying to hurry. It makes my stomach hurt to be sitting here while a child could be dying, but I don't know what else to do."

Rob took a swig of his beer, and set the bottle down. "I think we need to try to talk to her again. Like now."

"Agreed," I said, grabbing my bottle and starting for the stairs. Rob grabbed his and followed. TJ was still wrapped up in the movie.

I didn't wait to attempt contact. "Emma, we need you to talk to us. We can't find you if you don't help us. You need to hurry, too."

I was almost angry at the meager clues Emma provided. Why didn't she just come out with it? I had to kick myself to be patient. I guess it doesn't work that way.

I started when I felt the chill. "She's here," I whispered to Rob.

"Emma?"

She's going to die.

"Then help us, Emma. You're the only one who can. What did you mean by letters? What letters?"

They fall out of the bag on the floor. He steps on them sometimes.

"So, like mail?"

Yes.

"What about the man? Why does he have mail all over?"

His outfit.

"Outfit? You mean like a uniform?" Rob asked.

Yes.

Rob sat forward on the bed. "Is he a mailman?"

I think so. So many bags in his truck with letters stuffed inside and coming out the top. One fell on me.

"Emma! That's great. Thank you."

Hurry, she said again, and she was gone.

"What do you think?" I asked Rob.

"I think it's a solid start."

"How many mailmen are there around here? How many were here when Emma went missing?"

"I don't know, but this is the first real clue we've had. I'll go back to the office and search town records for our mail carriers, see if anything jumps out."

"If something does, we can search his house," I said, eager to find answers.

"Probably not. Not without a warrant, and I doubt I could get one without probable cause. Clues from a ghost wouldn't cut it."

"We'll deal with that problem when we come to it," I said, disappointed and feeling scared for Marilee. "For now, if you can research the mailmen, we'll figure out what to do from there."

I walked him to the front door and impulsively hugged him. His hands on my waist, he looked down at me and his eyes held mine. My stomach knotted up when his gaze moved to my mouth. The air around us seemed to stand still.

He cleared his throat. "I'll, uh, let you know if I find anything."

I stood looking at the door after he was gone. What was that?

I moved over to the couch and dropped down next to TJ. He grinned up at me and I ruffled his hair. It was easy to let my thoughts wander as I stared at the screen. And my thoughts were really wandering. Did Rob mean anything by it, that looking at my lips thing? Was it my imagination that the moment was loaded? Did I want Rob to have felt what I felt?

Something else occurred to me. It had been several days

PAMELA MCCORD

since I'd felt any guilt about Tom. About being disloyal to him by spending time with Rob.

But now wasn't the time to contemplate my feelings about Rob. Not with two little girls missing, one of them on the verge of death. It was the kind of event that puts things into perspective.

I sent TJ up to bed at the end of the *Avengers* movie. Restless, I tried switching channels, then picked up my Kindle. I hadn't been able to concentrate on reading since all the ghost stuff started. True to form, I still couldn't concentrate on it, so I moseyed out to the kitchen and collected the beer bottles to drop in recycling and wrapped up the leftover pizza and put it in the refrigerator.

It was still early, too early to go to bed, and I didn't know what to do with myself. Nothing came to mind, so I climbed the stairs to TJ's room and sat on the end of his bed. There was no chill in the air, no disturbance in the force, nothing to indicate Emma's presence.

"Emma," I whispered. "You don't have to talk to me, but I wanted you to know I'm here for you and Marilee. So maybe you won't feel so all alone."

After awhile, I headed for my own room. I lay back on the bed, hands under my head, and stared at the ceiling, unable to stop my thoughts from turning to Rob. Why now? In the middle of all that was happening. And what about TJ? I know he likes Rob, but he's too young to contemplate what that could mean if Rob and I—

Rob and I nothing. I couldn't have feelings for Rob. It wouldn't be right. It seemed like only yesterday that Tom was here. I owed it to him to be faithful to his memory.

What the hell? Hadn't I just reflected on the fact that I wasn't feeling guilty anymore?

CHAPTER 24

I must have dozed off, because I jumped when I heard my phone ding. I sat up and stretched. The phone dinged again and I pulled it out of my pocket.

It was Rob. I rubbed my eyes and answered, "Hey."

"I hope I didn't wake you. Sorry to call so late, but I have the information on the mail carriers. Marysville only has two. It's a small town after all. John Brindleson and Sara Kagle. Sara's been a carrier for three years. She replaced Tony Spencer, who passed away." He paused. "John Brindleson has been the mailman for 12 years."

"Twelve years? That's long enough—"

"I know."

"Do you know him? Do you know anything about him, what kind of man he is?"

"Sure, I know him. We don't hang out or anything, but I run into him now and then. He's always seemed nice. I only see him when he's in public, so I would expect him to be on good behavior."

"No rumors or anything?"

"Not really. He's been married for at least twenty years. Has a kid in college. As far as I know, he's an upstanding citizen."

My shoulders slumped. "Oh."

"I'll dig around. See if I can find anything on him."

"That would be good." I suddenly had a thought. "Do you have any pictures of him?"

"Not that I know of, but I'll check around. Why?"

"Because maybe . . . maybe Emma would recognize him if he was the one who took the girls."

"Good idea. I'll come up with something."

"Let me know as soon as you do."

I felt useless, and there wasn't time to be useless if we were going to save Marilee. If Rob found a good photo of the mailman, at least that was something. But, in the meantime, I hated feeling useless.

I HEARD THE ALARM GO OFF IN THE morning, but resisted opening my eyes, weighed down by despair over the seeming impossibility of the puzzle we had to solve. I threw an arm across my eyes and groaned. I was reluctant to face the day, until a brilliant plan burst to the surface of my brain and my eyes flew open. I threw back the covers as a wave of optimism propelled me out of bed.

I turned the plan over in my head while I brushed my teeth and got dressed. While I scrambled eggs and fried bacon for our breakfast. While I loaded the dishwasher. That's when a little doubt began to creep in. Who did I think I was, Nancy Drew?

I shook it off. This was going to work.

It was Saturday, so there was no camp. TJ played on his tablet and watched TV until, wanting more action, he went out to play in the backyard. Kate had installed a hoop on the side of the garage and TJ liked to practice his shots. I was vaguely aware of the sound of the basketball hitting the backboard. I puttered around in the kitchen, killing time, glancing out the backdoor at my son now and then, glad to have him out of sight of the front of the house.

At eleven fifteen, I positioned myself on the front porch swing with my Kindle, waiting. My nerves pretty much precluded any meaningful reading, but I'm pretty sure I looked like the real deal—simply a woman relaxing on her front porch.

Mr. Brindleson usually delivered our mail promptly at eleven thirty. He seldom deviated from his routine. This morning, I would talk to him.

He smiled and waved as he came up the front walk. I set my Kindle down and waved back.

"Nice day, isn't it?" I said in my most cheerful manner.

"Sure is." He stood on my porch as he sifted through the handful of letters he held, pulling out the ones addressed to me. "Would you like these?" he asked as he handed the packet to me.

I took them and smiled, not sure what I wanted to say, how to get where I needed to be.

"Looks like you got scratched up a little," he said, indicating the red marks on my arms. Just the opening I needed.

I laughed. "Unfortunately. I went hiking up at Bluebird Lake yesterday. Should have worn long sleeves."

"Might be a good idea for next time." He turned and started to step off the porch.

"It's, uh, it's beautiful up there, don't you think?"

He looked at me, an odd expression on his face. I never took the time to chat with him.

He shrugged. "We're lucky to live in such a gorgeous place."

"Do you ever do any hiking? I was thinking how fun it would be to have a cabin up there, on the water somewhere. But I wouldn't have any idea where to look."

"I'm sure you could find something. We have a few lakes around here you could check out."

"I suppose. Seems overwhelming. Do you know anyone who's bought something like that I could maybe talk to?"

He shifted his weight from one foot to another, relaxing a little, I hoped. "As a matter of fact, I have a cabin."

"Is it near the lake?"

"Right on the water. It has a dock and everything."

"Do you have a boat of your own?"

"Oh, yeah. It's a beauty. Good for fishing and any kind of water sports."

"Is yours on Bluebird?"

"No. One of the other lakes."

"Oh, which one?"

It might have been my imagination but I thought he looked suspicious. "Sorry. You don't have to tell me. I'm just being nosy."

He seemed to soften. "No problem. Bluebird's more expensive. You get a better deal on Backbone Lake or Cupid's Lake or one of the other ones. Of course, they're farther away. Not as convenient for a weekend jaunt."

"So you don't get to visit yours very often?"

"When I need to."

"Did you use a local realtor?"

"No. Cabin's been in my family for a long time. I inherited it from my father."

"I'm sure you enjoy it when you get a chance. I appreciate your tips on the other lakes." I stood and picked up my Kindle and my mail and turned to the front door. "Nice to talk to you."

He nodded, then looked behind me as TJ opened the screen door.

"Hello, young fella," Mr. Brindleson said.

"Hi," TJ said.

I felt a chill run up my spine. I stepped inside the door and said, "It's time for lunch. Go wash your hands." I nodded once again to the mailman then locked the screen door behind me.

My stomach was in knots at the thought a potential murderer had taken notice of my son.

I made a superhuman effort to disguise my shaking hands as I created TJ's favorite lunch of peanut butter and jelly with a glass of milk. I was too queasy to eat anything myself.

The mailman took little girls. He wouldn't be after my son. Would he? How could I have put my son in danger that way? It took a bunch of deep breaths before I got myself under control.

Rob called to say he wanted to bring over a couple of photos of Brindleson. I couldn't wait until he arrived.

I called out the backdoor for TJ to come in, and put the coffee on. I went upstairs and brushed my hair and checked that my face wasn't the pasty white I was sure it had been after my conversation with Mr. Brindleson.

When I came back down and glanced around, I didn't see TJ and called his name. When he didn't answer, I opened the backdoor and stepped outside. No sign of him in the yard. I hurried around the side of the house to the front, but still nothing. My heart jumped into my throat and panic started to fill up my brain as I rushed back to the backyard. The basketball lay in the grass at the edge of the paved area.

I ran back inside and upstairs to his room, which was empty, and checked everywhere, yelling for him. I could almost smell the fear cascading off me. My insides were clenched into a cramp.

Rob arrived while I was rechecking all the rooms.

"I brought the pictures so we can . . . ." He stopped when he saw my face. "What's wrong?"

"TJ's missing," I said, my voice trembling.

"Are you sure he's—"

"I've looked everywhere. The backyard, his room. The *whole house*. He's been taken."

"Why would you go there? Who would take—"

"Brindleson, that's who."

"Out of nowhere, he'd suddenly take your son? Why would he do that?"

"Because," I looked down. "When Brindleson came today, I thought it would be a good idea to see if I could get any information from him that might give us a clue, so I spent a few minutes chatting with him. And then TJ came out and Brindleson saw him and now TJ's gone."

He took my arm and steered me to the couch. "Tell me what happened with Brindleson."

I gulped a few deep breaths trying to get control of myself. Rob took both of my hands in his and squeezed them. "Take your time."

Tears started in my eyes, and I brushed at them. "He asked about my scratches." I held up my arm to demonstrate. "So I told him about going hiking and how nice it was and how I might want to buy a cabin on the lake. Then I asked him if he knew anybody with a cabin and he said he did. And I asked if it was on Bluebird Lake and he said no but didn't tell me which one. But he said he has a dock. And a boat."

"That's good information."

"He said he inherited the cabin from his father." My

hand flew to my mouth. "That must be where he took TJ!"

"First of all, we don't know he took TJ. TJ's a kid. He might have gone for a walk. We'll go see if we can find him."

"But if Brindleson—"

"If we can't find him ourselves, I'll investigate the Brindleson angle. For right now, though, let's go see if we can find him. Okay?"

I was more than grateful that Rob was here to help, and dared to have a speck of hope.

"Where was the last place you saw TJ?"

"He was in the backyard, shooting hoops."

"How long ago was that?"

"It was . . ." I paused. It hadn't even been an hour yet. "Twenty or thirty minutes maybe? By the time TJ finished his lunch, I thought Brindleson would have been long gone, so I wasn't worried."

"I don't want to minimize your concern, but twenty or thirty minutes isn't a long time for a kid to be missing."

I hung my head. "I know. It's just—"

"I know. You're understandably worried because of Brindleson, but it's too early to go there. Let's see if we can find TJ." He stood and extended a hand to help me to my feet. "Let's go check out back."

We wandered around the yard, Rob taking a close look at the area around the basketball hoop, and I opened the garage side door. We were greeted by the musty odor of a long closed-up space. There was a light switch on the wall by the door and I flipped it on. It provided much more illumination than I expected. I had barely stuck my head in here since we moved into the house. Now, I looked around. There was ample room for the car, and it was easy to see that Kate was a very organized person. Boxes were neatly stacked, tools carefully arranged on a workbench.

Rob did a token sweep of the garage, I'm sure for my benefit, and confirmed that TJ wasn't there.

He pointed toward the back-fence gate. "Where does that go?"

I looked at him, a hint of relief. "There's a creek."

"Kids like creeks," he said, taking my hand and pulling me toward the gate.

The creek stretched in either direction. Trees and brush lined the banks on each side, effectively blocking our view.

"Should we split up?" Rob asked me, but I shook my head.

"I want to go with you," I said.

"Let's head right. If there's no sign of him, we'll go back the other way."

He looked at my feet. "You might want to consider something more appropriate for tromping through the mud and debris."

I was wearing flip flops and could see his point. I raced back to the house and pulled on the hiking boots I'd worn to the lake and was back outside in three minutes.

The creek was wide and swiftly moving. Lots of stones on

the shoreline to maneuver around. After one slippery incident where my foot slid off a rock, Rob took my hand to steady me and didn't let go as we picked our way along the creek. Nothing indicated TJ had gone this way, until up ahead I spotted something orange on the bank, half in the water. I took off running, shouting over my shoulder that TJ had been wearing an orange T-shirt.

Rob caught up with me as I stood staring down at a waterlogged Fanta Orange Soda carton. He must have seen the anguish in my eyes because he pulled me into a hug.

"Come on. Let's go back the other way," he said.

He took my hand again and I followed him along the bank. A ways past our back gate, the creek veered to the right. I was afraid to see what was around the bend. Afraid TJ wouldn't be there, and afraid he would be. I slowed down. Rob could tell I was anxious, probably from the way I was trembling, so he put his arm around my shoulders and said, "It'll be okay" as we walked together past the stand of trees that blocked our view of the creek's path.

Again I spotted a flash of orange. Before I could react, I heard "Mom. Hey, Mom!" and my son, my wonderful son, was waving from the bank twenty yards ahead of us.

I ran to him and jerked him up into a bear hug. "TJ. Oh, my God. I've been worried sick."

He looked at me, a puzzled expression on his face. "I was just exploring the river."

"First of all, it's a creek, not a river." I hugged him again.

"Thank God." And then I started to cry. Rob was instantly at my side, his arms around me.

"What's wrong, Mom?" TJ asked, looking back and forth between me and Rob.

"Nothing *now*," I said. "When I couldn't find you anywhere, I panicked. You need to tell me if you're leaving the yard, especially if you're going down to the creek. I mean it." I tried to be stern, but relief overrode my anger as the anxiety left my system. "Come on. Grab your stuff. Let's go home."

"Aw, Mom. I was going to try out some of this fishing gear I found in the garage."

"I don't want you down here by yourself. It's not safe. Let's go."

He looked at Rob, who shrugged. "You're mom's right. If you want, I'd be happy to take you fishing sometime. We can sort out the gear you found in your garage. Okay, buddy?"

TJ's face reflected his inner conflict over doing what I said or arguing more, but he finally started picking up the fishing stuff, and gave Rob a sharp look. "Will you really take me fishing?"

"Absolutely," Rob responded, resting a hand on TJ's shoulder. "Here's a tip for you, bud. With your fair skin and light hair, you really need to wear a cap when you're out in the sun like this. Do you have one?"

"I've got a Yankee cap of my dad's," he said.

"That'll work. Especially if you remember to wear it."

I kicked off my muddy boots at the backdoor. "I need coffee."

"I could use a cup, too," Rob said.

As soon as TJ was out of sight up in his room, I slumped into a kitchen chair and buried my face in my hands. When Rob pulled me into his arms, I let him.

"I was really scared," I moaned. "When Brindleson looked at him, I stopped breathing. When I couldn't find TJ—"

He smoothed my hair, holding me against his chest. My heart was thumping so loud I was sure he could hear it.

"He's okay. You're okay, right?"

I pulled away and looked up at him, my eyes brimming with unshed tears. "I'm okay. But I don't think I would have been without you. I can't thank you enough for being here."

"You don't have to thank me. Of course I would be here."

I don't know why, but I blushed. To cover my emotional reaction to his words, I stood suddenly and moved to the sink, turning on the water, and turning it off again. I didn't even know why I was doing it. After a quick, apologetic glance at him, I removed a couple of mugs from the cupboard and poured coffee for both of us.

"This really helps," I said, sipping my coffee. "It'll take a minute before my adrenalin level drops." I stared into my mug, allowing the relief to flood over me, then suddenly remembering why he'd come by.

"Your pictures. We need to have Emma look at your

pictures." I set my mug down hard and stood. "We shouldn't be wasting time."

He carried his coffee and followed me into the front room. He'd left the folder with the photos on the couch. We retrieved it before heading upstairs.

TJ looked up from his comic book when he saw us at his door. "Mom?"

"It's okay, TJ," I said. "We just need to talk to Emma." I called for her as soon as I walked into the bedroom. "Emma, we need you. Come out."

I smiled at my son. "Can you run downstairs and get my coffee for me?" I asked, wanting him out of the room when I brought out the pictures. "And stick it in the microwave for 25 seconds too, okay?"

"But I want to talk to Emma, too," he whined.

"You can talk to her when you get back, buddy," Rob said.

I gave TJ a little shove and he slouched out the door.

Rob hovered in the doorway while I sat on the bed. Fairly quickly, the room grew cold and a breeze lifted my hair.

"Emma," I said. "We want to show you pictures of someone we think might be the man who took you and Marilee. Can you look at them?" I spread them out on the bed.

She didn't say anything. Rob and I exchanged worried looks. Maybe this wasn't going to work. Maybe Brindleson wasn't the right man.

A shriek filled the room. Rob's hand jerked and coffee

sloshed out of his mug. The breeze that had played softly with my hair took on the force of a hurricane.

Jumping to my feet, I said, "Emma! Stop! It's okay. It's just us, me and Rob, and we're trying to help you. Please."

"I think that's the answer we were looking for," Rob said, setting his mug on the dresser and looked around for something to mop up the floor, grabbing one of TJ's T-shirts I'd left on his bed for him to put away.

"It's him, isn't it, Emma," I yelled over the storm raging in TJ's bedroom.

Yessss came her answer as the wind died down. Sobbing came next, a heartbreaking sound.

"This helps us, Emma," Rob said. "Now we know where to start looking. Thank you for your help."

Hurry, she replied.

A thought came to me. "Emma, did you used to live in this house?"

No.

"Then why are you here? Why did you pick us to contact?"

You have my necklace.

"Your necklace?" I looked at Rob in confusion. "I don't—"

"The pendant," he said. "The one you bought from me?"

My hand went to my neck and I held the necklace out so she could see. "Is that what you meant, Emma?"

Yes.

"You lost it?"

It came off when the man stole me.

TJ got back in time to hear the conversation about the necklace. He looked around, his face scrunched up in disappointment as the chill disappeared. "She's gone?"

"I think so. Sorry, honey," I said. "Maybe next time she'll stick around longer." I took my coffee mug from his hand and rubbed his arm affectionately.

"Can I go watch TV?" he asked, sensing an opportunity to play on my guilt.

"For a little while," I said.

"We'll be down in a minute," Rob added to his departing back.

"Rob, your aunt said she found it somewhere. Red something. I don't remember what she said."

He looked thoughtful. "Red Creek Range?"

"Yeah, maybe. That sounds right. Is that on Bluebird Lake?"

"No, it's on Clarion Lake, an hour or so past Bluebird."

"Brindleson didn't mention Clarion. He suggested Cupid's Lake and Backbone. Maybe he didn't want me getting any ideas about where to find his cabin. Can we go there?"

"It covers a big area. I have an idea, though. I'll check property records and should be able to find the information I'm looking for. That'll make it too late to go up there today, so I'll go tomorrow."

"You mean *we'll* go up there tomorrow."

"You're not going with me."

"Oh, no, you don't." I pointed my finger at him. "It's because I bought the pendant that Emma told us about Brindleson. You can't leave me behind."

With a clenched jaw, Rob closed his eyes for a moment and sighed. "It could get dangerous."

"What if I'm willing to risk it?" I said.

"You have a son. Do you really want to risk your life?"

That stopped me, but just for a moment. "It wouldn't be dangerous if we knew Brindleson wasn't there. Emma said he's stopped coming. What are the chances he'd be there? Can't we get a warrant or something?"

"With what evidence?"

"Emma said the pendant was hers. We could show it to her parents and—"

"And tell them a ghost told you it was Emma's?"

I didn't have an argument for that. "I suppose that wouldn't work. Anyway, you'll be with me. It should be safe enough. It's not like I would be facing him alone, even if he was there."

He contemplated that for a moment, and I could see him wavering. Finally, he sighed again and nodded.

"Great," I said.

"And me?" a small voice piped up. TJ stood in the doorway. "I want to help find Emma and Marilee."

"I thought you wanted to watch TV," I said.

"I did, but I really wanted to hear what you guys were

talking about. And I want to go with you."

I exchanged glances with Rob. "I don't think so, honey. Sorry, but it's not a good idea."

"Aw, Mom." He humphed and crossed his arms to display his unhappiness at my words. "I'm not a little kid."

"You're right. You're kind of a medium kid. But I'm still not taking you on what could be a long, difficult trip."

"I don't even want your mom to go," Rob added, "but she's stubborn."

He gave me a rueful look. "I need to get back to the office. I've got some digging to do."

"I need to see if I can get someone to stay with TJ. I'll call Megan."

"Good. I'll call you later with details for tomorrow."

Punching in the babysitter's number, I hesitated. I didn't want TJ to be in the house without me, now that Mr. Brindleson knew about him. It wasn't a chance I was willing to take. Instead, I called Melissa, Kevin's mom, and arranged to drop TJ off in the morning. I owed her big time for coming through for me again.

Rob called after I'd sent my son up to bed. TJ was still bunking in my room, for both of our sakes.

"I checked property records and found the lot where Brindleson's cabin is probably located. At least, the property his father left him. It's on Clarion Lake."

"That's really, really promising," I said. "We might find her!"

"Don't get your hopes up. Nothing is certain. And, even if we do find her, she might not—"

"Don't say it. We can't go there. I'm going to believe we'll be in time. When are you coming by tomorrow?"

"Let's make it nine. Wear hiking boots."

"I got the memo last time," I chuckled. "Don't worry. I'll wear my hiking boots."

CHAPTER 25

B y the time Rob's truck pulled into my driveway the next morning, I'd stuffed my backpack with extra clothes and other items we might need and packed an ice chest with bottles of water and Gator Ade and sandwiches.

Rob carted the ice chest to his SUV and settled it in the back. When he picked up my backpack, he gave an exaggerated *oof* and asked what I had in there.

"Baby food," I said.

He looked at me quizzically.

"If we find her, I wanted to have something to feed her. I'm not sure she could eat anything solid. Gatorade is because it has electrolytes."

He gave me a thumbs-up and a smile, tossed my backpack in the backseat and held the passenger door open for me.

"How far is Clarion Lake?" I asked.

"It'll take us about two and a half to three hours to get there."

I shivered in anticipation, anxious to get on the road. "It's going to work," I said.

"Your lips to God's ears," he responded, giving my hand a squeeze.

The sun was blazing when we got to the lake a little before noon. The closer we got to our destination, the more excited we both were, in spite of trying to keep our expectations under control.

When the turnoff for Brindleson's cabin came into view, Rob pulled off the road and we approached on foot.

There was an old Blazer parked next to the cabin. Rob motioned for me to stay back, to which I made a face, but did as he asked. He moved silently through the trees until he reached the back of the cabin. Fortunately, there were no windows along that wall. Then, with his back against the side of the structure, he peered around the corner, but pulled back quickly as Brindleson appeared, carrying something wrapped in a sheet toward his boat.

I appeared at Rob's elbow. He started to shush me, then nodded toward Brindleson who was approaching the dock in front of his cabin.

"Mr. Brindleson, is that you?" I moved out into the open with a wave, hoping he read my expression as being surprised to see him.

He whipped toward me, his mouth open, and took a quick hop off the dock into his boat, struggling with the unwieldy bundle he carried.

It slipped from his arms to the floor of the boat and Rob

stepped up beside me, gun held down at his side. He pointed at the bundle with his other hand.

"What's in the boat?" Rob asked.

Brindleson spun around. "What are—"

"I heard a rumor you had a nice cabin up here on the lake. I thought I'd come check it out. So, what did you put in the boat?"

"It's none of your concern," he spat. "Unless you have a warrant, you have no business on my land."

"Do you have something to hide?" Rob asked, stepping in front of me.

"I'm not hiding anything, and unless you have a warrant, get off my property."

"Are you sure about that?"

The bundle in the boat moved slightly. Rob's attention was drawn to it and away from Brindleson, giving the mailman the opportunity to pull a gun from the back of his waistband.

"Rob, look out!" I screamed. Startled, Brindleson swung toward me and fired. The force of the bullet spun me around. My feet flew out from under me and I hit the ground hard, sucking in my breath as the searing pain in my shoulder radiated through my body. Rob shouted my name, and I heard more shots. I felt lightheaded but pushed to my feet, needing to get to him, my arm hanging limply at my side, blood dripping from my fingertips. They were scuffling in the dirt beside the dock, Brindleson straddling Rob and fighting for control of his gun.

"Rob!" I yelled, racing toward the two men. Brindleson punched Rob hard in the face and jerked the gun free.

I barreled into him the moment he aimed the gun at Rob's face, knocking him off Rob before he could fire. The gun skittered away and I struggled to hold Brindleson down as Rob scrambled to his knees and dove for the gun. Brindleson shoved me off, but Rob reached the gun an instant before Brindleson did. He stood and trained it on the mailman, then stooped to pull me up.

"Are you okay?" he asked, his eyes reflecting his worry. "You're bleeding."

"So are you," I said, noticing the bloom of red soaking his T-shirt.

"I'm okay. Go check the boat."

Reluctantly, I pulled my eyes away from him and, cradling my wounded arm, leaped into the boat and dropped next to the bundle, feeling movement when I touched it. Pulling aside the sheet, I found an unconscious child, pale and limp. I bent to check whether she was breathing.

"I have her!" I called. "She's alive, but I'm not sure for how long." Gritting my teeth at the pain in my shoulder, I scooped her into my arms, standing bracing my feet against the bobbing of the boat. I carefully stepped back onto the dock, and laid her down. I held two fingers against her neck, feeling for a pulse, and was alarmed by its weakness.

"I need you to get me a rope out of the truck," Rob called after giving me a couple of minutes with the frail child. "I need to secure Brindleson. Do you think you can you leave her for a minute?"

I looked back and forth between him and the child, calculating whether she'd be okay if I left her. Gently touching her face, I murmured to her that I'd be right back, I rushed to the truck and grabbed the rope for Rob. He handed me the gun and told me to cover him while he tied Brindleson up. I didn't have much experience with a firearm, but I'd seen a lot of movies so I managed to look competent until Rob finished.

Handing him back the gun, I grabbed a bottle of water and a Gatorade from the truck and rushed back to the little girl I'd left lying on the dock.

I heard Rob calling for backup and an ambulance as I cradled the child, smoothing her hair and speaking softly to her. She didn't respond, and I poured a little of the water on my hand and patted her face with it, hoping it would revive her. Kneeling in the dust of the dock, I raised her up with one arm and held the bottle of Gatorade to her lips and tipped it up slightly. At first, the liquid ran down both sides of her closed mouth, but then her lips worked and a little made it in. She seemed to savor the sip, but when she tried to swallow she sputtered and coughed.

Rob knelt beside us, and I was aware of him grimacing in pain with every move he made. My heart clenched, but Marilee's need was greater at the moment.

He leaned her forward and rubbed her back gently, which seemed to rouse her.

"Marilee," he said. "You're safe now. I'm a policeman. Can you hear me?"

She didn't respond and he called her name again. And then her arms went around his neck and she sunk against him. I breathed a sigh of relief.

"You're safe," Rob told her. "We're here to take you home."

She pulled her arms in close, tucked her hands up under her chin, and curled closer to him but didn't speak.

"Can you try to drink some Gatorade?" he asked. She lifted her head and looked at the bottle I held out to her. She moved her head toward the bottle and I held it while she took a few tentative sips. Letting Rob take over, I went back to the truck for the baby food and a spoon.

In the background, Brindleson shouted and threatened to sue. Rob growled a shut up and made a threat or two of his own. Worry about Marilee made it easy to tune out the mailman's rantings.

The child was filthy, and the stench of myriad bodily fluids floated in the air. I wanted to cry at the horrors she'd endured as I knelt beside the two of them, twisting open the jar. "If you can eat a little of this, it'll help you get stronger," I said. I scooped a spoonful of the banana mush and she opened her mouth just enough for me to insert the spoon, but she seemed too weak to take it off the spoon. I pulled it out of her mouth, gently scraping a tiny amount of the banana mixture off the spoon against her top teeth, then stroking her throat to help her swallow, which she finally did. But she turned her face away, back against Rob's chest. She refused any more attempts to get her to drink or eat, and all we could do was hold her and keep her calm until the ambulance arrived, followed closely by a couple of police units.

CHAPTER 26

I felt profound relief at the sound of sirens. An ambulance crunched gravel under its tires as it ground to a stop near the dock. Cops and paramedics gathered around Marilee, who was still cradled in Rob's arms, gently separating the little girl and allowing Rob to stand. One of the paramedics expressed concern about the blood on Marilee, but I assured him it was Rob's blood. Two of the police officers took custody of Brindleson, bundling him into the back of one of the cruisers after determining he wasn't injured, while another officer conferred with Rob. The paramedics lifted Marilee onto a gurney and did a check of her vitals, pronouncing her dehydrated and malnourished. They started a fluid IV drip and loaded her into the ambulance. When the paramedics attempted to tend to me and Rob, we insisted they get Marilee to the hospital and worry about us after she was taken care of. They weren't having it and said that, until we let them check us out, they couldn't leave. Rob told them in no uncertain terms he'd already let dispatch know there was an officer down and another ambulance was en route. He said more police were on the way to secure the crime scene.

"Look, you're wasting time. My wound isn't life-threatening, but Marilee's in a lot worse shape than I am, or Kelly is. We'll be okay here until the other ambulance arrives. You need to get that little girl to the hospital now."

He held up his hand to ward off the argument he could see coming. The lead paramedic shook his head in exasperation and pulled a supply of bandages and alcohol wipes out of the back of the ambulance and shoved them at Rob. "Put some pressure on that wound so you don't bleed out," he said, slamming the door. "I hope you know what you're doing. It's on you, man."

"Do you think—" I started, concerned about Rob's condition, but he cut me off.

"I'm fine for now. Can you do a quick and dirty patch job?"

His face was pale and he swayed on his feet as he watched the ambulance back out of the driveway and pull away once it hit the main road. He breathed in sharply, squeezing his eyes shut as a spasm of pain shook him. His arm went around my shoulders. At first I thought it was to comfort me, but when I felt him slump against me I realized he needed me to hold him up. The red stain on the bottom front of his shirt was spreading. I lowered him down to the dock and sat beside him. When I tried to lift up his T-shirt, he stopped me. "I'm okay." He touched my hand. "I'll be okay. Don't worry about me."

His hands were covered in blood. "You're *not* okay," I said.

"For now, I am. I've been shot before, and I can tell this one is fixable. It's just super painful."

He did seem like he was rallying, and color was coming back into his face. "It hurts like a bitch, though," he said, with a short laugh.

The laugh calmed me down. He was strong. Maybe I didn't need to be afraid for him. But I took the bandages and wipes from him and ripped one of the packages of gauze open. I waved his hand away when he tried to stop me from using it to slow the bleeding. He finally dropped his arms and let me do it. "Happy now?" he had the nerve to ask.

"I will be once the other ambulance gets here." I picked up one of his hands and put it on the bandage so he could keep the pressure on the wound.

I picked up the discarded wrapper for the gauze from the dock beside me and crumpled it into a ball. Suddenly, unexpectedly, reality set in and hit me like a ton of bricks and I started to hyperventilate.

"Are you okay?" Rob asked, his voice rising in alarm. "Come on. We can drive ourselves to the hospital." He stood carefully and offered his hand to help me up, but I shook my head so he sat back down on the dock beside me. "What is it?"

I gulped in a breath, trying to stop the trembling that had taken over my body. He rubbed my good arm, worry plastered all over his face. "What is it?" he asked again.

"Rob." I gulped again. "Rob, if we'd been five minutes later . . . five minutes . . . we wouldn't have been in time. If I'd drug my feet getting TJ to his friend's house, if we'd stopped for gas. So many things could have gone wrong."

"But they didn't. We *were* in time. Marilee is safe. We saved her."

I heard his words, but wasn't comforted. The *what ifs* swirled in my head. Silent tears coursed down my cheeks, and Rob hovered, looking helpless. Finally, he put his arm around me and I buried my face in his chest, my hiccupping sobs releasing all the fear and anguish I'd been holding in.

When I stopped shaking, he held me away from him, careful of my wounded arm.

"I feel the same horror that we could have been too late. But I can't give in to that horror. Kelly, it can haunt you if you let it. We saved that little girl. You and I did that. You need to focus on that and be content that things turned out the way they did. This was a good day."

I looked at him without speaking for a moment, and shuddered as I shook off the shroud of gloom that had settled over me. "Okay. I'm okay now." I stood and gathered up the bandages. "Let me clean up that wound." After a moment, he got to his feet and followed me into Brindleson's cabin.

One of the officers from the second police unit stood on the porch. He put up a hand to stop us, but the determined look I gave him caused him to back down, with an admonition that it was a crime scene. Rob assured him he'd make sure we were careful.

The door wasn't locked and inside blinds at the windows were drawn closed, leaving the interior dim. Opening the blinds, I was surprised to find the cabin was meticulously tidy. Not what I would have expected given what Brindleson probably used the cabin for. I motioned for Rob to follow me to the kitchen, pulling out a chair for him.

He was starting to look pale again. The blood on the front of his shirt had spread and was soaking into his jeans, and I felt an urgency to stop the bleeding before he passed out. The piece of gauze had fallen off somewhere between the dock and the kitchen. I tried as gently as I could to pull his T-shirt off over his head, but I could tell the motion hurt him, and he gritted his teeth against the pain.

"We shouldn't be in here," he said. "This is a crime scene."

"I heard the cop outside, but I don't care if it's a crime scene. You're losing blood and I need to do something about that."

He protested, but weakly. I washed my hands in the sink, rinsing the blood from my shoulder down the drain. It still seeped, but I wouldn't think about that now.

The officer stood in the kitchen doorway watching us, and nodded as I used a paper towel to pull open one drawer after another so I wouldn't add my fingerprints to the scene while I looked for clean dish towels. During the search, I found a big bowl, which I filled with warm water. Grabbing one of the dish towels and submerging it in the bowl, I wrung it out and used it to clean up the blood around Rob's wound, then held the dish towel against his abdomen for a minute to staunch the blood flow. I used a second one to dry the area, and opened one of the alcohol wipes to disinfect his injury. He sucked in his breath, but didn't let out so much as a groan as I applied a bandage and taped it on.

I handed him a bottle of water from the refrigerator, using another paper towel on the refrigerator handle. Rob was starting to look better. I wanted him to sit quietly for a few minutes, but he would have none of it.

"Now, let me fix your arm," he said. I started to decline the offer, but gave in when I saw the determination on his face.

My T-shirt was short-sleeved so all he had to do was push up the sleeve to expose the hole in my upper arm the bullet had left as it tore through. The bleeding had mostly stopped. He found another dishcloth and used it to clean the residue off my arm, and then wiped the wound with alcohol. He worked diligently and efficiently, no doubt the result of his training in the Marines.

When he was done, we sat at the kitchen table. It was weird, being in a monster's house.

The officer who'd been hovering in the doorway wandered outside once he decided we weren't going to do any harm to the crime scene.

The two of us were a mess, both covered in blood. There

would be no saving our T-shirts. "You look like hell," I said with a laugh.

"You're not so pristine yourself," he responded with a crooked grin. "And I'm sorry I got my blood all over you."

I shook my head. "I'll send you the bill." After a moment, I said, "Should we search this place to see where he was keeping her?"

"No. It might compromise any evidence if you touch anything else. The forensics team is already going to have a fit over us coming in, let alone using stuff from the house."

"You can't cut me out of this." I watched his reaction, but he didn't seem to be persuaded. "Come on. It's not fair. I shed blood over this case."

He reached across the table and took my hand. "Yes, you did. And you saved my life."

"Just call me Wonder Woman," I said with a grin. "I'm really glad I saved you, but I still want to take a look around."

When he accepted that I wouldn't be dissuaded, he said, "You can watch me, but you can't touch anything," and pushed up from the table.

He took the lead, and I followed, careful not to disturb the scene. The cabin wasn't large. Just a kitchen, living room, small bath and one bedroom. Rob did a cursory sweep of the living area, but there was nothing to point to a kidnapped child being held here. We left the cabin by the front door and headed around the side. I stopped to wipe the sweat off my forehead, glancing around the area.

"There!" I pointed to a weeping willow on the bank of the lake about ten yards away from the cabin, and took off at a run.

"Wait!" he called after me, but I didn't slow up. "Don't touch anything."

"I won't," I yelled over my shoulder. When I got near the tree, I spotted a structure at the base of the trunk, partially concealed by the drooping branches of the willow. The structure had bars, and its door was standing open. It was like an animal cage.

Rob joined me and leaned in to inspect the enclosure. Then drew back as the stink hit him. The floor of the cage had splotches of excrement and other dried on substances which might have been blood or vomit or urine. God knows what that little girl had endured. I could only hope that she'd been unconscious and unaware of the filth boxed in with her.

"I think there should be plenty of her DNA to prove that's where he was keeping her." We both stood and stared, unable to look away as our imaginations called up images too ugly to bear.

"There was no cover, nothing to protect her from the elements. Not even a tarp. Thank God the cage was under the branches of the tree so it might have given her some relief from the heat. But they wouldn't have protected her from rain or cold or insects." I shuddered.

Rob rubbed a hand over his pale face. "Come on. Let's go."

I put my hand on his arm. "We need to find Emma."

He looked at me and nodded. "I know. Emma is the reason we found Marilee. We owe her. But—"

The sound of the ambulance pulling into the drive interrupted him, and we headed back toward the cabin.

"Don't worry. Our investigators will go over every inch of this property. If she's here, we'll find her." He slipped his arm around my shoulders, and I leaned against him as we walked.

The EMTs loaded Rob into the ambulance and I climbed in with him.

"Will they take us to the same hospital as Marilee?" I asked.

"Yeah," one of the EMTs answered. "We're going to Carden General. It's the closest and set up for trauma patients."

I silently prayed that Marilee was going to make it. She'd been so weak, and she'd endured so much. My eyes burned as I begged God to take care of her.

Rob reached over and held my hand. Now that we were safe, my mind whirled with thoughts of him and the feelings he elicited from me. I'm not sure when it happened, but I became accepting of the idea that he was going to be in my life, even if we hadn't talked about it. He wouldn't want to push me and would leave it up to me where we went from here, but I knew he cared for me. And I cared for him. I squeezed his hand. He looked up at me and our eyes met and held. What we saw in each other's eyes told us everything we needed to know.

He nodded off and slept the rest of the way to the hospital. I didn't let go of his hand. When we arrived, I stepped out first and waited for him to be unloaded. He woke up when the EMTs jostled the gurney out of the ambulance.

Inside, there was a buzz in the air. Over her clipboard, the admitting nurse said to me, "Thank God you found that child. How did you do it?"

Suddenly the consequences of our actions dawned on me. Brindleson could say we searched without a warrant. Maybe the charges against him would be thrown out. What could we say, that a ghost told us where to go?

"It was dumb luck," I finally responded. Rob and I needed to discuss our statements, and we needed to do it soon.

"Whatever," she said, smiling and patting my arm. "It must have been God guiding your steps." She nodded to someone over my shoulder and another nurse appeared and motioned me toward an empty bay. I wanted to stay with Rob, but nurses rule the ER, so I followed my nurse.

She chattered about the press in the main hospital. This would be a huge story and I expected the fallout would land on me and Rob before long.

"You're a lucky girl," the nurse said. "The bullet missed anything important. You're going to be sore for a few days, but you should be back to normal before you know it."

"That's good to know," I said. "What about Marilee? Do you know anything about how she's doing?"

"Not yet, but I'll see what I can find out. You two are heroes."

"We're not important. That little girl is. I just hope we were in time."

"She was alive when she was brought in. We've got top-notch doctors here. She's in good hands."

"Can you find out about Rob, too?"

"Sure, honey."

She ambled out of my bay. I lay on the bed reflecting on all that had happened over the course of the day. I'd finally let go of my dark thoughts about not being in time to save Marilee. For now. Rob was right. It was a good day. My attention turned to him. He'd been pale and weak, but hadn't collapsed, despite having lost a ton of blood. Adrenalin had kept him going long past when he shouldn't have even been able to stand.

The nurse pulled back the curtain, a bright smile on her face. "Your boyfriend's stable. They've given him a transfusion, and his doctor wants to keep him overnight, but he's gonna be fine. And so far that little girl is hanging on. They flushed her with liquids and nutrients and her color is better. She hasn't been awake, though, since they brought her in. But I've got a feeling she's gonna pull through." She pulled open the curtain around my bay, turning to confirm that I was free to go but should come back tomorrow to have my wound checked. She intended to bring a wheelchair for me, but I nixed that idea strongly enough that she didn't push it.

I thanked her and picked up my backpack. I wanted to find Rob. The nurse's words finally registered. *Your boyfriend's stable.* I no longer had the inclination to fight back against my feelings. I liked that she referred to him as my boyfriend. Even if he really wasn't.

The desk directed me to Rob's bay where a few uniformed officers were milling around outside while a doctor and nurse were inside with him. One of the policemen noticed me, and my bandaged arm, and extended his hand.

"You must be Rob's friend Kelly?" The other cops gathered around me when I nodded, making sure I was okay and offering bits of information they'd managed to pick up.

"Have you been in to see him?" I asked the first one, who'd introduced himself as Mickey Root.

He looked sheepish. "No one was in his room when we got to the ER so we invited ourselves in. We were only in there ten minutes or so before the doc came in and booted us out. Rob wasn't awake while we were in there."

"I overheard the nurse say his vitals are good and strong. The doc didn't seem real concerned while he was in there," said a second cop. "I'm Daniel, by the way."

"Hi, Daniel. He was moving around while we were at the cabin. Other than looking pale and a little peaked, I wasn't afraid he wouldn't make it. He did bleed a ton, though."

"Yeah, they had a couple of blood bags hanging by his bed," Daniel said.

"The press is going to find a way to get in here," Mickey said. "They don't know the whole story yet, but they'll dig until they get it. Then they'll be gunning for you two."

"How *did* you guys know where to find Marilee?" a third cop asked.

I didn't know how to answer that and, luckily, the doctor took that moment to step out of the bay. He took in all our expectant faces and said "Things look good. I see no reason why Det. Porter won't be back on his feet in a week or so."

A cheer went up among the police officers. And me. I cheered right along with them. I dared to hope that everything would turn out all right.

"Are you his wife?" the doctor asked me.

All eyes turned my way.

"No. I'm his . . . friend."

I noticed the looks passing among his visitors, but no one commented.

"Can we see him now," Daniel asked.

"No more than two should be in there at a time, and keep the visits short. He needs to rest."

I held back, not wanting to be hurried when I got my turn, because I planned to stay.

CHAPTER 27

The visitor's lounge was on the other side of the hospital, and it was thankfully empty, allowing me to relax and let go of the day for a few minutes. I pulled my cell out of my pocket and called Melissa to check up on TJ.

"They're fine," Melissa said. "In fact, the boys are angling for a sleepover. Is it okay with you if TJ spends the night? I can bring him home in the morning."

"You're sure you're okay to keep him overnight?"

"Yeah. Kevin's older brother Nate used to have his friends stay over when he was Kevin's age, so I'm an old hand at this. Not to mention that TJ keeps Kevin entertained so I don't have to." Melissa laughed. "Bad mom."

"Not bad mom. You're a lifesaver. I won't complain about having a night to myself. Thank you so much."

I heaved a sigh of relief, since I intended to spend the night in Rob's room.

Next, I texted Jen. *Have you got a minute?*

She responded immediately with *Sure. What do you need?*

I'm calling you.

"What's going on?" she asked as soon as she picked up.

"I don't know where to begin. First, I guess I should tell you I'm at the hospital."

"Are you all right? Is TJ all right?"

"TJ's staying at Kevin's tonight. Rob's in the ER and I'm staying here with him."

"Which one? I'm coming over."

"You may want to reconsider. We're at Carden and it's more than an hour out of Marysville."

"I don't care. I'll make Jason come with me. Save us a seat."

Her ability to lighten the mood made me laugh. "Okay. I could use the company."

"I forgot to ask. Is Rob okay? What happened?"

"He will be. I'll tell you everything when you get here."

"Okay, but maybe you could give me a tiny little hint?"

"Maybe I'll give you one if you bring me a blanket. It's freezing in here."

"Hospitals usually are. I'll take care of it. Now. The hint?"

"Check the news. I'm sure it's all over the TV."

"Ooh. I can't wait!"

I settled back on the marginally comfortable waiting room couch and closed my eyes, and must have fallen asleep because I woke with a start to someone calling my name. I rubbed my eyes and tried to focus on the man in blue standing in front of me.

"I thought you should know Rob's been moved to his own room, up on two," Mickey said. "Sorry if we made you feel left out. We've all been in to see him, so if you want a turn, you can have him to yourself now."

"I appreciate it," I said. "How long was I out?"

"Only an hour or so. At least that's how long it's been since we last saw you."

"Thanks, Mickey," I said, standing and stretching. "How did he seem?"

"He's still pretty out of it. He came around for a few minutes, and smiled, but then was out again."

"He's been through a lot today. He probably needs to rest as much as he can."

"I could say that about you, too."

"I'm sure I look ghastly," I said ruefully.

"Not at all. But I know you were with Rob and you got shot, too. Given all that, you look like Miss America to us."

"Thanks. Nice to know I won't scare him when I go in there."

"Oh, I'm pretty sure he'll be happy to see you. You mean a lot to him."

I looked at him, feeling a heat that I hoped didn't show on my face. "I do?"

He cleared his throat. "I mean, uh, I'm sure he'll be happy to see you."

I glanced at him, but he didn't meet my gaze as he walked with me to the second floor.

The other guys were standing around outside Rob's room and smiled when we walked up, every face alight with relief that Rob was going to recover.

"He's all yours," Daniel said.

He positioned one of the chairs next to the bed for me, then nodded and left me alone with Rob.

I settled into the chair and picked up Rob's hand. He didn't wake up, and I didn't know if he'd been sedated or was just asleep. I held his hand and thought about holding his hand. I looked at our hands together and I felt peaceful. Almost like I believed Tom would approve.

How close we'd come. Not just to being too late to save Marilee, but how close Brindleson had come to killing Rob. I started to shake at the thought of it. Losing this man would have destroyed me. I couldn't bear to lose him, too. I looked at Rob lying there, eyes closed, and thought about curling up next to him.

He opened his eyes, startling me out of my reverie. He looked at me and smiled a tight smile. "Thank God you're all right," he said, his voice groggy.

"Thank God *you're* all right. I was starting to get worried."

He tried to laugh, and grimaced in pain. "I shouldn't do that for a while."

"I won't say anything funny for two weeks," I deadpanned, pretending to scowl.

He chuckled softly. "Don't make any promises you can't

keep." He tried to shift, causing another spasm of pain, before he settled back into his original position.

"Aren't they giving you pain meds?" I asked, hating that he was still suffering.

"Yeah. Otherwise it would be a lot worse."

"Maybe they should up the dose," I kidded.

"Is there any news on Marilee?" Rob asked, searching my face.

"I think she's holding on. They were trying to get liquids and nutrients in her. That should make her stronger. But I haven't heard anything concrete."

"You're holding my hand," he said, his eyes searching mine.

"Yes, I am. Is that okay with you?"

"It's more than okay."

Squeezing his hand, I felt a yearning that had been missing from my life for a long time. I was in jeopardy of losing it, and closed my eyes until I could gain control of my emotions.

I cleared my throat and changed the subject. "Rob, we need to get our stories straight about how we found Marilee."

"Oh, yeah. You have a point. It's gonna be tough coming up with something that sounds plausible."

"I've been thinking. I talked to Brindleson about finding a house on a lake. What if we were exploring Clarion Lake and just happened on that dirt road leading to his cabin.

When we walked up to it, we saw him carrying something heavy that was moving. Then he started shooting."

"It's shaky," he said, "but it could work if we stick to it."

"Okay then. One problem down."

"We have more?"

"I've been warned that the press is going to be all over us. I'm surprised they haven't found us yet."

"We'll cross that bridge when we have to," he said. "I can't wait to get out of here. Did the doctor say when I can leave?"

"He said he wanted to keep you another day or two."

"That doesn't make me very happy."

"Oh, don't grouse. You're alive. Besides, I'll be here."

"You will?"

"There's no place I'd rather be."

"Thank you," he said, then his eyes closed and he was asleep again.

Looking at our hands together, I felt happy.

A sound from the doorway broke into my thoughts, and I looked up to see Jen and Jason. I stood as Jen rushed toward me. She pulled up short when she saw my bandaged arm.

"What happened to you?" she asked in alarm. "And what happened to Rob? Is he okay?"

"We're both okay. Let's go to the visitor's lounge and let him sleep."

The three of us made it as far as the visitors lounge door before Jen grabbed my arm and looked at me expectantly. "Spill."

A laugh escaped before I could stop it. "I don't even know where to start. You watched the news?"

"You mean the Marilee Harmon story?"

"Yeah, that one."

"She's here, isn't she? Coming through the lobby, we about tripped over all the paparazzi. There's going to be a news briefing in half an hour or so."

"Really? I want to see that. I haven't seen any of the news. What did the TV say happened?"

"That Marilee was rescued, and there was a shootout. It said two people were wounded."

"No names or anything?"

"No. I wasn't sure why—" She narrowed her eyes at me. "Wait a minute. Don't tell me it was you two."

"Guilty as charged."

"Tell us everything!'

"It's complicated. I'm not sure you'll believe me."

"Why wouldn't we? You saved Marilee!"

"I know, but—"

"But what?" Jen looked at me like she was frustrated by how long it was taking me to get to the point. "You've been shot! You're standing here in front of me with a bullet hole in your arm. *Of course* we'll believe you."

I started to tell her, but suddenly feared the real story getting out . . . getting back to Rob's boss. So I changed directions.

"I decided it would be fun to have a cabin on a lake. It's

so pretty up there. You know, Clarion Lake."

"So?" Jen raised her shoulders and tilted her head. "What does that have to do with finding Marilee?"

I cleared my throat. "Well, um, so Mr. Brindleson told me about his cabin and how much there was to do at the lake. That gave me the idea to see if I could find one I could afford. It would be great for TJ." I didn't look straight at her, afraid she could see my story was a tall tale. "Anyway, I looked on realtor.com and did some research on the different lakes around here. Rob was kind enough to drive up to Clarion Lake with me."

Jen raised a questioning eyebrow. "Really? You haven't mentioned anything to me about wanting a lake house."

Prickly sweat was creeping up my back. I'm not great at fibbing. I picked at a speck of blood on the bottom of my T-shirt. And Jen waited for me to continue.

"It was spur of the moment. Having a cabin on a lake seemed like a pipe dream, but I thought it would be fun to go look at what was available, so we drove up there and poked around. We stumbled on a dirt road that looked promising and decided to see where it would lead. We followed it to where it ended. At a cabin. We started to turn around because we didn't want to trespass, but right then we spotted someone walking toward the dock carrying a bundle. A moving bundle. That's how we found her."

"What happened then?" Jen looked skeptical, rubbing her chin with one hand.

Jason had been leaning against the wall outside the visitors lounge, listening.

"I'm sorry, Kelly," he said, pushing off the wall, "but I'm not sure I buy it. You're too fidgety and don't want to look at us."

Jen had those raised eyebrows going on. "He's right," she said. "Your story doesn't ring true. If you don't want to tell us about it, just say so."

Groaning, I said, "I do want to tell you. Everything. But you won't believe me."

"Why?" Jen asked. "You found Marilee."

"Yeah. But we didn't do it alone. We had help."

"From?"

I couldn't help dragging it out. How could I tell them that a ghost led the way?

"You can't tell anyone about this." I ushered her and Jason into the visitors lounge and closed the door behind us. "It would be really bad for Rob if you did."

"What are you talking about? You and Rob saved that little girl. He's a hero. No one's going to—"

"They would if they found out a ghost told us where to look."

Jason's face screwed up in a *give me a break* grimace. Even Jen looked confused.

I took a deep breath. "Jen, I told you about the night we spent in a hotel after weird things happened in TJ's room. And you made me tell Rob about it. At first, he was skeptical, too. But he then saw it, heard it, for himself. In fact, he installed a nanny cam in TJ's room to document it."

Neither said a word, but Jen's mouth was hanging open.

"I told you how the ghost was crying and asking for help. Well, we decided to ask what it wanted. It turned out the ghost is a little girl named Emma who was kidnapped years ago by the same guy who took Marilee. Who happens to be our mailman, Mr. Brindleson."

Jen waved her hands wildly. "Wait a minute. Mr. *Brindleson?*"

"Yes. Mr. Brindleson. Anyway, Emma gave us clues about where we could find Marilee. She told us Marilee didn't have much time left. Brindleson had stopped going out to his cabin where he had her in a cage. And he'd stopped bringing her food and water. Emma's the one who pointed us toward him. Thanks to her, we got there in time. Brindleson was just carrying Marilee, wrapped in a sheet, out to his boat when we spotted him. I think he was going to dump her in the lake."

"How awful!" Jen said. "But a ghost? Wow."

"Kelly, I'm sorry, but I'm having a hard time swallowing this," Jason said.

"I figured you would. I probably wouldn't believe it myself if I hadn't experienced it."

We all looked at each other, at a loss. Finally, I said, "You can ask Rob about it, but only when you're alone with him. I'm pretty sure he won't want the real facts getting around, especially to his superiors. That wouldn't be a good thing." I stood. "Look, I know this sounds preposterous. Ask Rob. He'll confirm all of it."

Jen's mouth flattened in a thin line. She was clearly in a state of *I don't know what to make of this*. "Can we say hi to him?"

"We can go see if he's awake."

Back in Rob's room, Jen pointed to the TV. "I think the press conference is going to start soon. Should we watch it?"

"Yeah," I said, and switched the TV on. Rob was still out, so I kept the volume low.

There were still five minutes before the press conference was due to start. The three of us sat in the chairs on each side of the bed, waiting to see what information would be released.

"He looks really pale," Jen said. "Is he going to be okay?"

"He lost a lot of blood, but the doctor said he was lucky. The bullet didn't hit anything vital. He might get discharged tomorrow or the next day."

Our voices were low, but after a couple of minutes Rob opened his eyes, squinting at the light in the room. "Kelly?" he said.

"I'm here, Rob. Jen and Jason are here, too. They came to see how you're doing."

With effort, he turned his head and groaned in pain. "Hey, you guys," he croaked, his voice hinting at a dry, scratchy throat. "Did Kelly tell you what happened?"

"Kind of. It was a pretty strange story, dude," Jason said.

Rob tried a small chuckle. "Tell me about it."

Jen leaned over the bed and rubbed his hand. "How are you feeling? You poor thing."

"I'm okay," he said weakly. "Did she tell you she saved my life?" He glanced at me and smiled.

"No. We haven't heard the whole story yet. They're doing a press conference. I think it's about to start."

"Can't wait to see what they have to say," Rob said.

CHAPTER 28

The press conference was being held at the hospital entrance, and a crowd had gathered around the microphone stand. Rob's boss, Harold Magnusson, made his way to the mic, nodding to dignitaries along the way, receiving pats on the back. When he reached the mark, he cleared his throat and introduced the parents, the mayor, a doctor and a few members of the task force who had been investigating Marilee's disappearance.

"Today, Marilee Harmon was rescued. She's being treated here at the hospital and her doctor will fill you in shortly. The suspect has been arrested on kidnapping and other charges."

He was interrupted by several reporters shouting questions about the identity of the suspect, but Chief Magnusson declined to release Brindleson's name. He continued with the narrative, mentioning there was a shootout and that a detective and a civilian were wounded. Thankfully, he also declined to release Rob and my names, but indicated that none of the wounds were life-threatening.

The doctor was up next. He had upgraded Marilee's condition to stable. She was responding well to the nutrients and liquids she was receiving intravenously. She wasn't awake yet, but indications were good that she would recover fully.

"God, that's a relief," I said. "I still haven't stopped freaking out over how close we came to not being in time."

"I know. But we were."

"So, how did you save Rob's life?" Jen asked.

"She tackled Brindleson before he could shoot me again," Rob said. "I owe you one," he directed at me.

"Buddy, tell me this isn't really a ghost story," Jason said quietly.

"Wish I could, Jas, but sometimes truth is stranger than fiction. Just make sure the true story doesn't leave this room."

"We're gonna have a beer and you're gonna fill me in on this," Jason said. "I'll give you a week to recover, then you and me are gonna have a talk."

"I'll tell you everything but, seriously, man, this can't get out or I'll be a joke at the station."

When Rob looked like he could hardly keep his eyes open, Jen and Jason said goodnight and said they'd check in with me tomorrow to see if there was anything they could do to help.

I took a minute to call TJ and wish him goodnight. He didn't mention Marilee but I needed to ask him to keep the story quiet. I could say nothing now and wait to talk to him when he came home tomorrow, but what if he saw it on the news tonight? Was it worth the risk?

Finally, I said, "Honey, I just wanted you to know that we found Marilee today, and she's alive."

He squealed in excitement and I could hear voices in the background.

"Listen, you haven't, you know, told anyone about Emma, have you?"

"No, Mom. You told me not to."

"Could you still not tell anyone? I don't think they'd believe you and they might think ... I don't know but they just wouldn't understand. So, don't tell, okay?"

"Okay, Mom. See you tomorrow."

"Have a good night, honey."

CHAPTER 29

I stepped out of the bathroom in Rob's room the next morning, surprised to find him awake. "Hey," I said.

"Hey," he said back.

He still looked so tired. Despite what the doctor had said, I couldn't help worrying, but Rob assured me that he felt much better than the day before.

"Captain Magnusson wants to take my statement," he said. "I guess we should go over our story again."

"Yeah, we should. Do you think our story about looking at lakefront property will hold up to scrutiny?" I asked.

"Maybe, but they'll wonder why I was with you."

"Because we're friends?"

"Yeah. Friends." His eyes searched mine, and I had to look away to keep him from seeing the flush rising in my face.

"Well, that part's true, at least," I said. "And I think it's plausible. After all, we did go to Bluebird Lake. They just don't know we were on a mission and not on a—"

"Date?" His eyes crinkled as he smiled at me.

"It wasn't a date." I was growing uncomfortable, although I wasn't sure why. Cold feet, maybe?

"Of course it wasn't."

"No, I didn't mean—"

Before I could continue, someone said "Hello" and I turned to see a man and woman of about my age standing in the doorway.

The man stepped forward, his hand extended. "We hate to intrude. We're Marilee's parents, Jane and Nick, and wanted to thank you for bringing our daughter back to us."

"Oh." I stood quickly and moved to take his hand. "I'm Kelly Harris, and this is Rob Porter."

Jane rushed forward and grabbed me in a hug, which I returned and started to cry.

She was crying, too. "We can never thank you enough for what you did for us."

"You don't need to thank us. We were just lucky to be in the right place at the right time." I shrugged a little as I wiped my eyes.

"I think I'm going to be sobbing for days," she said, smiling.

Rob shifted to sit up further and the Harmons moved to his bedside. Nick shook hands with him. "There are no words to convey our thanks to you. Both of you. I'm sorry you had to get shot while rescuing Marilee."

"It comes with the job sometimes," Rob replied.

Having been around Rob enough to know he was feeling uncomfortable with the outpouring of gratitude, I indicated the two chairs to take the focus off him. "Why don't you sit down for a minute."

Jane started to speak but was overcome with emotion and put her hand over her mouth. A hiccupping sob escaped. "I'm sorry," she said. "I can't seem to get control of myself. We were afraid we'd never see her again."

I bent and put my arms around her shoulders. "Don't apologize. I understand. I have a son, and I'd be devastated if anything happened to him. Just let the happy thoughts sweep over you. You can't change what happened, but you shouldn't dwell on the negative. Yesterday was a good day."

"Kelly's right," Rob said. "The *what ifs* can drive you crazy. I think fate led us to your daughter. It was meant to be."

"Thank you. Those words help."

"And I agree with Kelly," Rob said. "You don't owe us anything. Concentrate on getting Marilee healthy again."

We all turned toward the doorway at the sound of someone clearing his throat.

"Captain Magnusson," Nick said. "We just wanted to thank Rob and Kelly for saving Marilee."

"Mr. Harmon. Sorry to intrude, but I have some questions for Detective Porter. Would you mind excusing us?"

"Of course not," Nick said as he slipped an arm around Jane's waist and escorted her from the room.

"Do you want me to go, too?" I asked.

"That won't be necessary. I have some questions for you as well."

"Sounds ominous," I said, but took a seat by the bed.

"I wanted to get your statement. Do you feel up to it?" he asked Rob.

"Of course, Captain."

"First, what were you doing at Mr. Brindleson's property? You didn't have a warrant, I presume."

"Uh," Rob started.

"He was helping me check out lakefront properties," I said.

Captain Magnusson shot me a look. "Lakefront properties. Hmm."

"Yes," Rob said. "It was pure luck that we stumbled on Brindleson carrying Marilee out to his boat."

"We were driving and spotted a dirt road that looked like it went down to the lake, so I asked Rob if he'd go that way. He parked and we walked toward the lake and that's when we saw Brindleson with what looked like a bunch of sheets in his arms." I watched the captain's eyes as I spoke. "And then he put it in the boat and the pile of sheets moved and Rob yelled out what's going on or something like that. That's when Brindleson shot me."

"He'd put Marilee in the boat. When he heard us coming, he pulled out a gun and started shooting."

"That's fairly convenient, wouldn't you say? I mean, you just happened to pick the dirt road that ended at Brindleson's cabin, and he just happened to pick that moment to carry her out to the boat?"

"Yeah. Lucky for us. I think God sent us there," I said, making my eyes wide.

"God. Okaay," Magnusson said. "So, you both got shot and you still managed to take down Brindleson?"

"It wasn't as easy as that," Rob said. "He shot Kelly and I pulled my gun and returned fire but he was already moving. He got off a shot at me and headed for the boat. I jumped him and tried to take his gun away. Kelly piled into him and threw him off balance and we were able to overpower him. Then Kelly ran to the boat and found Marilee. I called it in. That's about the extent of it."

"Uh huh." Captain Magnusson seemed skeptical but said, "When you're up to it, come in and type up your report."

"Do you want to ask me any questions?" I asked. He looked at me for a long moment, and shook his head.

"We'll be talking," he said to Rob on his way to the door.

"Captain?" Rob said and Magnusson turned back. "I think maybe you should send a team out there and see if you can find anything else. We don't know if Marilee was his only victim. Can you just check?"

Magnusson nodded. Then he was gone.

"Was that too easy?" I asked.

"Maybe. We have to wait to see what Brindleson's story is. Whether it raises any questions."

"He has to remember that I asked him about properties on the lake. Told him I thought I wanted to find one, so that supports our story. I mean, really, it's very plausible why we were there. And Melissa knew we went to Bluebird first because she watched TJ for me. No one can account for our miraculous timing."

"Can you get me some water?" he asked, and I poured him a glass from the blue plastic pitcher on the standing tray pushed out of the way against a wall.

"I'm surprised Brindleson was at the lake," I said over my shoulder. "I didn't expect him to be there."

"I've been thinking about that. The only thing I can come up with is that your questions raised an alarm for him and he decided to clean up loose ends."

"Loose ends? You mean Marilee."

"Yeah."

I gritted my teeth to stop them from chattering as a chill ran down my back. With a sob, I said, "He was going to kill her . . . because of me."

"Stop, Kelly. Stop. You can't think that way. First of all, he always planned to kill her. He was starving her and she wouldn't have lasted much longer as it was. Second, it's only because of you that we found her at all. Come on, don't cry. It's because of you that she's alive." He looked like he was about to try to get out of bed and I rushed to his side, almost spilling the water I was carrying.

"Stay there. I'm okay." I wiped my eyes and sat down next to the bed, suddenly feeling awkward. "I'm sorry. I know I'm being weird." I handed him the glass of water. "How do you feel?" I asked, fighting to keep any more tears from falling.

He peered at me, frowning for a moment, then his face relaxed. "I think I'm better than I was."

"The doctor said you might be released today. Do you feel like it would be too soon?"

"Hell, no. Being stuck in this bed is torture. If I'm going to be lying around, I'd rather do it at home."

In another example of miraculous timing, the doctor stuck his head in, a cheery smile on his face. "How are we feeling today?"

"Not bad. When can I get out of here?"

The doctor frowned. "I'd like to keep you one more night."

"I'd rather recover at home. I'm okay. Some pain, but it's manageable. I've been up this morning to use the bathroom and didn't have any problems with balance or anything. So, can you spring me?"

"Do you have anyone to stay with you at home? I don't think being alone, at least for tonight, is a good idea."

"No, I—"

"He can stay with me tonight. I'll keep an eye on him," I said quickly, before my brain could kick in with all the reasons it would be a bad idea.

Rob looked at me as if I'd sprouted a second head. I smiled and nodded.

"Okay. If she's okay with it. Does this mean you're letting me out?"

"I'll start the paperwork. You should be free in an hour."

He took a step toward the door, and turned back. "I just want to thank you, and you, Ms. Harris, for what you did yesterday."

"Could we see her? Marilee, I mean?" I asked.

"I think that could be arranged. Take care."

With the doctor having left, I suddenly felt embarrassed, barely able to meet the question in Rob's eyes.

"What?" I asked defensively.

"Nothing. Just surprised. I mean—"

"If you're bent out of shape over the 'date' word, I didn't mean it the way you took it."

"Really."

"No, I didn't. I just meant maybe we wouldn't want people to get the wrong idea."

"The wrong idea."

"Yeah, the wrong idea. I mean, we aren't dating as far as I know. If we are, let me in on it."

"I thought you weren't ready for, you know, anything."

"I did say that. Yes. But things change sometimes."

Glaring at him, I stood. "Why are you making a big deal out of this?"

"Me? You're the one who's focused on the word 'date.' Obviously, it's a big deal to you. And, I have to say, you're putting out mixed signals. What is it you want?"

"I don't *want* anything. I simply said I'd be happy to watch you overnight since the doctor seemed to think it was important for you not to be alone. If you don't want to, that's fine, too."

He didn't say anything for a long moment, and attempted a crooked grin. "Our second slumber party."

It also took me a moment to shake off the remnants of the dance we were engaged in. But, looking at his face, seeing the softening of his eyes, I let my anger go. "Doesn't mean we're going to make this a recurring event."

"I wouldn't dream of it," he said with a smile.

CHAPTER 30

With Rob's discharge papers in hand, he was ready to make a beeline out of the hospital, with a detour to see Marilee on the way. I walked slowly, in case he needed a hand, and reached the elevator first. When we stepped off the elevator on the third floor, it was obvious which room was Marilee's. A multitude of people were milling around the waiting area, a few in the hallway outside, and I looked questioningly at Rob. "Should we do this or make a break for it?"

"We'll have to face them sometime. Let's get it over with."

I hoped that we would be unnoticed. I was wearing the sweatshirt Jen had brought, and Rob was in a pair of sweats I'd purchased in the gift shop since his clothes were blood-stained and ruined. There was nothing to indicate we were the wounded heroes.

A few heads turned to scrutinize us when we drew near the door to Marilee's room. We ignored the looks and stepped inside. Jane looked up from where she sat beside Marilee's bed and beamed a hello.

Turning to her daughter, she said, "Marilee, these kind people saved you. This is Kelly Harris and Rob Porter."

Marilee's face split into a huge grin, and she held out her arms to me. I, of course, rushed to embrace her, sitting on her bed.

"I remember you," she said.

"I didn't think you were awake," I said, "but I'm happy you remember us."

People in the hallway outside the room, realizing who we were, swarmed the doorway, and Nick and a nurse shooed them out and closed the door. I shot him a thankful smile.

"The man took me," Marilee said, matter-of-factly. "I was afraid, but then you came."

"That man is in jail," Rob said. "He can't hurt you or any other little girl ever again."

She looked up at him with big, expressive eyes.

"How are you feeling, sweetie?" I asked, stroking her hair. "We've been thinking about you and hoping you were better."

"I'm not scared anymore. Thank you for saving me," she said solemnly.

"You're welcome. We're really happy we found you." I cradled her in my arms, her head on my chest.

She said something I didn't quite hear, and I bent my head closer. "What did you say, honey?"

"I said, I'm sad."

"You are? Why are you sad?" I asked.

"Because Emma's alone now."

Everyone's heads whipped around. "Who's Emma?" her mother asked.

"You know, don't you," she said to me.

I held my breath, not knowing what to do.

"Emma is my friend. She talked to me when I was scared."

"I know Emma is very happy that you're safe."

"Will you tell her?"

"Of course, we will."

Jane was looking at me, her face a question mark. "Who is Emma?"

"Can we talk about that later?" I asked.

She looked skeptical, but nodded.

Rob stepped closer and knelt by the bed, grimacing at the pain. "Marilee, I'm Rob. I wanted to tell you it's wonderful to meet you."

Marilee smiled a small, embarrassed smile. "I like you," she said.

He laughed. "I like you, too. I hope that, when you're home again, Kelly and I can take you out for ice cream sometime. Would you like that?"

"I would *love* that," she said.

The nurse cleared her throat. "Marilee needs her rest now."

Rob and I looked at each other, and stood. I squeezed Marilee's hand. "I'll see you soon, okay?"

She nodded as she scooted down, her head on the pillow.

Rob handed Nick his card. "If you need anything, please feel free to call me. I'm sure you have questions."

Nick thanked him, and Rob and I prepared to meet the onslaught waiting on the other side of the door.

Rob opened the door and extended his arm to clear people out of our way. Cameras flashed in our faces and he slipped an arm around me, trying to shield me from the press.

"It's an ongoing investigation and I can't talk about it," he responded to the questions shouted by the crowd, snaking our way through it. "No comment," he said as the questions didn't stop.

It seemed that the paparazzi intended to follow us all the way out of the hospital, but the nurse had the foresight to call for security, and they held back the crowd to give us a chance to escape.

We rushed through the hospital, choosing to leave by way of the emergency room, in case more reporters were waiting at the front entrance.

"I guess we'll have to go to your house later to pick up some clothes and stuff?" I asked, helping him into the car while the Uber driver held the door.

"Sounds good. I could use a toothbrush."

I laughed. "I'm with you on that. I'd *kill* for a toothbrush."

Rob leaned his head back against the seat and closed his eyes, his hand finding mine.

I looked down at our hands, but didn't pull away. Instead,

I slumped down next to him and closed my eyes, not aware of anything until the driver announced we'd reached our destination.

The driver carried my backpack up to the porch, while I helped Rob maneuver the porch steps. It was a relief to be home, away from the hospital and inquiring minds.

Opening the door, I offered Rob my arm and led him inside, depositing him in a comfy chair in the living room.

"I don't think you'll want to navigate stairs if you don't have to. Why don't I make up the couch for you to sleep on? Will that be okay?"

"Wherever you think is fine with me," he said. "I'm just thankful you offered to take me in for a night."

"Lucky for you, there's a three-quarter bathroom down here. And the kitchen, in case you get hungry." I carried in our things. "Can I get you something to drink?"

"Yeah, I'd love a beer."

"I'm sure you would, but I doubt your doctor would approve. Let's stick with coffee or tea."

"Coffee, then." He frowned dramatically. "Spoilsport," he muttered under his breath.

I laughed as I went to put the coffee on. When it was finished brewing, I poured two mugs and carried them into the living room, sitting on the couch.

"Ahh, the simple pleasures," I said, taking a sip. I was on my second sip when I heard a car pull up out front.

"That's probably Melissa bringing TJ home," I said,

opening the door in time to see TJ rushing up the path.

I waved to Melissa and watched a minute as her car pulled away. TJ had already discovered Rob was in the house and gave me a quick, but solid, hug, before heading to the couch to join Rob.

My son and his hero-worship. This time his hero was real.

I left the two guys to bond and went upstairs to get bedding for Rob and carried it back down, depositing it at one end of the couch. It was too early to make up the bed. TJ was bouncing up and down on it at the moment in his excitement at hearing the story from Rob. I sat beside TJ to listen, too.

"I wish I could tell Mike and Kevin," TJ said when Rob finished.

"I know, honey, but they might tease you. Not everyone gets the chance to talk to a ghost, and most people don't even believe they exist."

"But we can tell them ghosts are real."

"It's not that easy, honey. We can't prove it, so they'd probably think we were either making it up or genuinely certifiable."

"Certifiable?"

"It means crazy. Maybe someday you can tell them, but it would be great if you could keep it our secret, at least for now. Can you do that?"

"I guess. But it's so cool."

"It is cool."

"Can I tell them you and Rob saved Marilee?"

"Sure, you can tell them that. It's all over the news anyway. Just tell them your mom was looking for a house on the lake when she and Rob accidentally caught Mr. Brindleson with Marilee. That's a pretty cool story, too."

"Yeah! I can't wait to tell them!"

I ruffled his hair. My little sweetie.

"We should go tell Emma," TJ said excitedly.

"You're right," I said. "But let's do it later. Maybe by then Rob will feel like he can make it up the stairs. I'm sure he'd like to be there, too."

"You shouldn't wait," Rob said. "She deserves to know."

"Can we, Mom?"

"I guess." I looked at Rob. He nodded toward the stairs.

"Wait," TJ said. "Did you find Emma, too?"

"No," Rob said. "But I asked the police to search the area for other victims. Hopefully, if she's there, they'll find her."

"I hope so. I feel sad for Emma."

"Us, too," I said. "Come on, let's go talk to her."

He scurried to catch up with me as I climbed the stairs, and raced ahead of me into his room.

"Emma!" he called.

He waited a minute, looking around, and dropped his head in disappointment. "She's not here."

"No, I don't think she is," I said. "It's not cold in here like it is when she visits."

"Emma!" he called again louder. "Emma! My mom and Rob saved Marilee. She's in the hospital."

He looked at me, concern on his face. "Where is she?"

"I don't know, honey. We'll try again later."

"Okay." He brightened. "Hey, can I sleep in here tonight? She might come back."

"I guess if you want to. It's your room, after all."

"I'm going to stay up here right now, just in case."

"Sure thing. I have to go do something about dinner. I'll call you when it's ready."

I debated between pasta and pizza on the way down the stairs. Pasta I'd make and pizza would be delivered. Pizza was looking better and better as I thought about how tired I was, even if it would be the second or third time we'd had it in the last week.

"What happened," Rob asked as soon as he spotted me coming down the stairs.

"Absolutely nothing. Emma wasn't there. TJ's very disappointed."

"So am I. Maybe her job is done and she was able to leave."

"That would be nice, but if that was the case then why was she hanging around all those years before Marilee was kidnapped?"

"Huh. I guess it's a mystery."

I flopped down on the couch. "Pizza okay with you?"

"Sure. I'm easy."

"I appreciate it. Although, please accept my apology as that's pretty much all you get to eat around here."

He laughed, then squeezed his eyes shut over the sudden pain.

I grimaced, sorry for the pain he was in.

"If you make a list of things you want from your house, TJ and I can go pick them up for you."

"I hate for you to have to go to all that trouble."

"Seriously? You should stop worrying about putting me out. We'll be back before you know it."

"I'm not sure. It might be okay, but there might be dishes in the sink." He winked.

I rolled my eyes. "You think you're so funny." Tossing a pillow on one end of the couch, I patted it. "Make yourself comfortable. We'll be back shortly."

CHAPTER 31

Since I'd already been to Rob's, it didn't take long to throw clothes and toiletries into a duffel bag I found on his closet floor. I'd left TJ in the front room, TV on, while I packed Rob's stuff.

I had a moment of panic as I tried to block thoughts about whether I'd made a mistake inviting Rob to stay with me. It made sense but, now that I was away from him, it dawned on me that we'd be together in such intimate circumstances. I'd be taking care of him, alone with him. And I wasn't sure how I felt about that. On the other hand, I'd be taking care of him, alone with him. I chuckled at myself.

Pushing back the anxiety, I lugged the duffel back to the living room. "Ready, buddy?"

On the drive home, I hoped TJ couldn't hear my heart, which was beating so loudly I could barely hear myself think.

I had to smile when I opened the door to see Rob asleep on the couch. Maybe I'd worried for nothing.

He lifted his head when he heard us, and gingerly sat up, rubbing his eyes. "I wasn't really sleeping. Just resting my eyes."

I shook my head and dropped the duffel bag by the couch.

"Help me up?" he asked, holding out his hand. I grabbed it and pulled him to his feet.

He shuffled into the bathroom and I sat down to wait. When he returned, the front of his hair was wet where'd he'd splashed water on his face.

Something had occurred to me. "So, Marilee could see Emma."

"I know. That's really freaky. This whole thing has hit me hard. I never believed in ghosts, or even the afterlife, before. It's a little hard to discount it now."

"I know what you mean. I was ambivalent about it. I didn't *not* believe in ghosts, but I never thought I'd actually see one. Not that we saw Emma, but you know what I mean."

"Yeah. I hope the investigators find her, so she can rest in peace."

"How long do you think it will take before we hear anything?" I asked, tucking my legs up underneath me.

"I think they'll have the whole area covered by the end of tomorrow. They'll put several cops on it. Maybe when we go up there tomorrow . . . Can you take me to get my truck?"

"Sure. If we wait until after I drop TJ off at camp."

"We don't have to go at the crack of dawn. It'll take two or three hours to get there and, the later we turn up, the more time the investigators will have had to turn something up."

OF COURSE, TJ WOULD BE disappointed we were leaving him behind. But it was a crime scene we were going to and an exuberant kid running around might not be the best for preserving any evidence, not to mention we had no idea what the police may have unearthed.

I was putting the coffee on when I heard Rob stir. I wandered into the living room with a cheery *Good Morning*. He groaned as he tried to sit up, finally turning onto his side and sliding his feet off the couch.

I could sympathize. Every little movement I made was painful, and everything I did took longer, because, well, I was in pain.

"Need some help?" I asked.

"I think I've got this. I *hope* I've got this." With a grimace, he righted himself until he was in a sitting position. "Hurts like a bitch this morning," he said through gritted teeth.

"Mine does, too, but I'm sure not as much as yours. Pain really takes the energy out of you."

"Yeah."

"I put clean towels in the downstairs bathroom, and your travel pack is in there, too. There's a walk-in shower, in case you can manage it. If you even want to."

"Probably should make an effort. I feel grungy. Those sponge baths they give in the hospital aren't really satisfying."

"I imagine they're not. Listen, while you're in getting ready, I'll make some bacon and eggs. There's no hurry. I don't need to drop TJ off for camp until nine, so take as long as you want."

"Thanks," he said, stiffly getting to his feet. It took him a moment to feel steady before he shambled toward the bathroom, one painful step at a time.

I woke up TJ for breakfast, watching as he stretched and yawned.

"She didn't come," he mumbled sleepily. "I tried to stay awake, but I couldn't. She would have woken me up, wouldn't she?" he asked.

"I'm pretty sure she would. Maybe she needs a little time to get used to being alone again."

"But, Mom, she wouldn't have to be alone. *We're* here."

"I don't think it's the same, honey, but I'm sure she knows we're here for her. Give her some time."

I ushered him toward the bathroom. I'd washed my face and brushed my teeth before I went downstairs the first time. Now, I pulled my hair up into a messy bun and changed out of the PJs, robe and slippers I'd been wearing and into jeans and a tank top.

The smell of bacon and eggs brought both Rob and TJ into the kitchen. Rob was still moving slowly, but looked better after a shower.

Both of us still felt the effects of the days before, with our aches, pains and exhaustion. Moving around should take some of the kinks out. Or so I hoped.

Rob and I dropped TJ off at the Methodist church and watched as he greeted his friends and climbed on the bus that would take the kids to camp. I waved once more as we pulled out of the parking lot and settled in for the drive to Clarion Lake.

We didn't talk a lot the first twenty minutes. Rob sat slumped in his seat, looking out the window. Once or twice, I glanced at him wondering if he was all right.

Finally, I said, "You're deep in thought."

"Sorry. I didn't mean to ignore you. My brain is spinning with all the supernatural things we've been dealing with. I mean, *ghosts*?"

"Yeah. I don't think I'll ever look at life the same way again. Never in a million years would I have believed what we just went through was possible."

"And what about when Marilee asked about Emma? As odd as it seems, it felt normal ... ish ... when you and I talked to Emma, but to find out we weren't the only ones knocked me for a loop. I don't know how to process it. I'm used to trying to make puzzle pieces fit. These pieces don't fit any puzzle I've ever seen."

"We should write a book. Of course, we'd have to market it as fiction."

He laughed. "What? You think no one would believe us?"

THERE WERE SEVERAL POLICE CARS In the clearing in front of the cabin. When we parked and got out, an officer approached us, hand outstretched.

"Rob. God, am I glad you're okay."

Rob gave his hand a shake. "Jim, I want you to meet Kelly Harris. Kelly, this is Jim Santos."

I shook the extended hand. "Have you had any luck finding Em . . . I mean, were there any other bodies?"

I looked at Rob. "Sorry, I couldn't wait to find out."

He laughed and turned to Jim. "We've been wondering if Marilee was the only victim."

"No problem. There's nothing to indicate there were any others. We're about to wrap up here. We've collected samples from the cages under the tree for DNA testing but, unless it shows otherwise, I think she was the only one."

"Oh," I said, trying to mask my disappointment. "Well, we're just here to pick up Rob's truck. Don't want to keep you."

Rob looked at me then nodded at Jim. "I'll talk to you later, man. Let me know if you find anything."

"No problem."

"I'm sorry," I said as we made our way to Rob's truck. "I shouldn't have been so impatient. Do you want to stay?"

"No, I don't think there's much I can do here that they can't."

"You're coming back to my house, aren't you?"

"Yeah. At least to pick up my stuff."

"Okay, I'll follow you."

———————————————————————

HE PULLED UP TO THE CURB AND I parked at the side of the house. I watched him get out of the car, checking to see if he needed help but, despite his slow pace, he seemed to be capable of making it to the front door.

I let us in and headed to the kitchen to put on the coffee. Rob had flopped down on the couch. Driving while wounded could really take it out of you, and we were both exhausted. Coffee might help. If not, I'd suggest a caffeine IV.

I set the mugs on the coffee table and sank onto the couch next to him. Picking up my mug, I clinked his and said "Cheers."

He laughed, grimacing when the pain hit, but gamely leaned forward to clink back.

"Are you going home tonight?" I asked, watching him sip his coffee.

"I probably should. I appreciate you watching out for me last night, but I don't want to take advantage."

"It actually is no problem, and I think you should stay. For one thing, the less you have to do for yourself the quicker you'll get better. Also, I think we should make another attempt to contact Emma, and you might not be up to facing the stairs until tomorrow."

He frowned, seeming to contemplate what I'd said.

"It's up to you, of course," I said.

"Got a couple of Tylenol?" he asked.

I stood and took a step toward the kitchen.

"I'm too sore to move anyway," he said. "I'd love to stay if you really don't mind."

"I don't mind at all."

I brought back the pain pills and a glass of water, then sat down on the couch and picked up my coffee. It felt good to just relax.

Setting my cup down, I leaned my head back against the cushions. Until I remembered I needed to pick up TJ from camp.

"Take it easy. I'm going to get TJ and will be back in a few minutes."

He started to rise, but I put a hand on his shoulder to stop him. "Just relax. Okay?"

I grabbed my bag and keys and felt him watching me as I left.

CHAPTER 32

TJ bounced into the house ahead of me. "Maybe Emma will talk to us today. Can we go up to my room?"

He paused. "Hi, Rob. Are you coming with us?"

"TJ, give us a few minutes to visit before you drag us upstairs," I said. "Rob needs to rest."

"Oh, okay," he said with the just slightest hint of disappointment in his voice.

"Hey, buddy," Rob said. "Did you have fun at camp today?"

"Yeah! But I wished I could tell my friends all about Emma." He looked at me. "Mom said I couldn't."

"I know, but not everyone will understand," Rob said. "Is it so bad for the three of us to have a secret?"

"I guess not." He shrugged, and brightened. "Actually, it's kinda cool."

"That it is," Rob chuckled. "We'll go up in a few minutes. I'm not sure Emma will come through, though. She didn't yesterday. I hope she shows up, but don't be too disappointed if she doesn't. Maybe she's just sad right now."

"But then we won't be able to talk to her."

"I know. We just have to wait and see."

I went into the kitchen to refresh Rob's and my cups.

"What happened when you went back to the cabin?" TJ asked.

"Not a thing. They're almost done with the search for additional victims but haven't turned up anything," Rob said.

"So we stayed about ten minutes then drove back," I added.

"But you didn't find Emma?"

"No, unfortunately," I said. "Emma's remains are up there somewhere and I don't think she can move on until they're discovered. So, we'll try really hard to find her."

"That's really sad."

"I know, honey. That's why she's probably still around, and we're hoping she can help us find her." I took a sip of my coffee, feeling as dejected as TJ.

Rob cleared his throat. "I heard from one of my neighbors while you were gone. Apparently, the paparazzi are camped out at my condo."

"Oh, God. I forgot about them. I wonder why they're not here, too."

"I don't think the department has released your name yet. Or maybe they think I'm more important." He said that with a grin and a grimace.

"You deserved that," I said, grinning back, resisting the urge to poke him in the side. "It seems like it's a good thing you're hanging out here so they can't find you."

"You're probably right. Maybe in another day or two they'll move on to the next story and forget about us."

"This is a pretty big story, so don't hold your breath."

"I'll just keep ducking them."

"Or maybe you should give them a statement so they can move on."

"I'd just be telling them that I can't comment on an ongoing investigation."

"Yeah. Go with that."

"You may be right. I'll arrange to speak to the press at the station so maybe they'll stop waiting for me at my house."

TJ was a little gnat flitting around, anxious to get up to his room and, hopefully, his ghost. He practically sent up a cheer when I set down my mug and stood, and he darted for the stairs.

Poor guy couldn't understand why I didn't dart, too.

TJ was bouncing on the end of his bed when I got to his bedroom.

"Can I call her, Mom?"

"Go for it," I responded.

TJ's chest puffed out proudly and he looked at the Dot. "Emma, are you here?" He looked around the room when she didn't answer. "Emma, can you come out? We want to talk to you."

Nothing happened. TJ's face fell and he looked at me like I could help. Which I couldn't.

We sat quietly waiting for ten minutes. "Sorry, honey, I

don't think she's coming today." I put my arm around his shoulders. Of course he shook me off.

He stood. "I don't know why she—"

A soft sobbing came from Alexa as the room grew cold. TJ drew in a breath and pointed excitedly. "She's here," he whispered.

"Are you okay, Emma?" I asked.

The crying grew louder. "We're here, honey. Don't be sad."

TJ called down to Rob. "Emma's here!"

I wasn't surprised when he came limping into the bedroom a minute later, holding his side.

"We saved Marilee, Emma. She's going to be okay," I said. "Thanks to you."

The sobbing stopped. *I know.*

"Emma," Rob said. "Can you tell us where you are? We want to find you, too."

There was silence for a whole minute.

You won't ever find me. He put me in the water.

I gasped and put my hand over my mouth, tears filling my eyes.

"Then we'll look in the water. We'll find you and you can be free to leave that place."

No one can help me.

The room grew warm again and she was gone.

Rob pulled me up into his arms. "We won't give up. I promise."

He let me go, and I wiped my eyes with the bottom of my T-shirt.

"How, Rob? How can we find her if she's in the lake? We don't have any idea how far out he might have taken her."

"We'll ask Emma if she can give us some clue about where to look."

I sank back down on the bed. Rob gently sat next to me. "Are you okay?" he asked.

"I'm just discouraged." I wiped my eyes again. "I was so sure that when we found Marilee we'd find Emma. So she could go into the light. It wouldn't be fair if she saved Marilee and then we couldn't help her."

I sighed and stood up. "I don't think Emma's coming back anytime soon, so why don't we go back downstairs where the coffee is."

Shooting TJ a look, I said, "Want to help me get dinner going?"

He hung his head and grumbled "I guess."

"Maybe tomorrow will be better, buddy." I pulled him in a hug, knowing he was as disappointed as I was.

I couldn't help feeling sorry for Rob when I saw the pained look on his face as he contemplated facing the stairs.

"I know it's still early, but you could stay up here if you want and I can bring dinner up for you. TJ can sleep in my room tonight and you can have his."

Maybe he actually considered my offer, but he responded with, "Thanks, but I've already put you out enough. I can make it downstairs." He started for the door to preclude my arguing with him.

I kept my mouth shut as I watched him painfully navigate his way down. His knuckles were white as he gripped the bannister.

"You're kind of a mess," I said when he'd settled back on the couch. "I feel sorry for you."

He grinned. "I can't lie. I feel sorry for myself. You wouldn't think one little hole in your side could hurt this much."

"I would," I said. "My little hole is in my arm."

Rob and I l bumped fists.

TJ HAD SLUMPED UP TO BED after dinner, as disappointed as Rob and I were. It was hard to shake off the gloom at what Emma had said.

Carrying our mugs, Rob and I moved into the family room, each letting out a groan of pain as we carefully sat down side by side on the couch.

We sipped our coffee in silence until Rob sat forward abruptly.

"I have an idea. It's a long-shot, but maybe I can parlay my 'hero' status into getting a favor from the department. I'm going to asked Captain Magnusson to drag the lake."

"Will he do it?" I asked.

"It's a big job, and so far there's no reason for him to think Brindleson had more than one victim, so it'll be a hard sell. But I can say that we stopped him as he was about to take Marilee out in the boat, and we believe he was going to dump her in the lake. It's thin but, like I said, my stock is up after the rescue so maybe I can pull it off."

My heart jumped into my throat and I teared up as I gazed into his gray eyes. He put his hand over mine. "It's only an idea, and I don't know if it will work.

"But at least it's *something.*"

I threw up my hands in mock exasperation. "What are you waiting for? Call your captain!"

"I might have more luck if I make my request in person," he said. "You know, give him the old wounded hero hang dog look. I'll go in tomorrow morning and meet with him."

"I'm not going to be able to sleep tonight," I said and stood up. "But it's getting late. Why don't you let me make up the couch?"

He nodded and moved to a chair while I spread the sheet across the cushions and plopped a pillow on one end and a folded blanket at the other end.

As he limped toward the couch, I impulsively threw my arms around his neck. Momentarily surprised, his arms went around me and we stood together until I kissed his cheek and let him go.

He looked down at me. "What was that for?"

"You're a good man, Rob Porter," I said.

He moved closer as if he meant to kiss me, and I held my breath, but he stopped and smiled awkwardly. "So," he said. "See you in the morning?"

I must have looked silly standing there with my mouth hanging open. I cleared my throat and stepped back. "Yeah. I'll see you in the morning."

He watched me walk away, and I glanced back at him as I headed up the stairs, our eyes still connected when I vanished from his sight.

My heart was beating loudly as I closed my bedroom door and leaned against it. What was happening to me? When my breathing was normal again, I headed down the hall and stuck my head in to check on TJ, who was already asleep.

There might be more than one reason I wouldn't get any sleep tonight.

CHAPTER 33

It was after 4 p.m. by the time Rob got back the next afternoon, and I'd already picked up TJ from camp. I waited for the coffee to be done, anxious to hear the results of Rob's meeting with his boss.

"Captain Magnusson grudgingly agreed to send out some divers. He felt the need to point out that it was pretty flimsy reasoning on my part but, hey, he's going for it. I think it helped when I mentioned an older missing child case . . . a little girl named Emma Corning."

"I'm so relieved," I said. "I've been a bundle of nerves all day. It almost makes me want to bake him cookies."

"You can bake me cookies anytime," Rob said with a smile. "I think Captain Magnusson might be immune to your efforts to sweeten the deal."

He paused for a moment, and cleared his throat. "I'm going to be part of the search team."

"But you're not okay." I said.

"I'll be okay enough."

"Have you done that kind of search before?"

PAMELA MCCORD

"I had Marine Combat Diver training. So, yeah. I know what I'm doing."

"You're really going out with them?"

"I'm planning on it."

"But you're not up to your . . . your—"

"My superpowers?"

"Yeah. Your superpowers. You know what I mean. You're still recuperating. Won't your injury inhibit your swimming ability?"

"I've been wounded before. I can tough it out."

"But the water's dirty. What if your wound gets infected?"

"I'll have a waterproof dressing put on the wound. That will keep the bacteria from getting in. I'm going to be there to find Emma."

I didn't have an answer for that. I just looked at him in frustration.

"Does your captain know you're planning to join the search?"

"Uh, no. I'll talk to him about it tomorrow. It'll be fine. I'll make sure of it."

I sipped my coffee, fighting to rein in my anxiety. "You're staying tonight, aren't you?"

"Do you want me to?"

"I don't want you to overtax yourself if you're planning to dive in two days."

"Aren't you sick of me yet?"

"I want you to be healthy enough that you don't join Emma down there."

"Aww. You care."

"You're impossible!" Though I was frustrated with him, I had to laugh.

"Oh, I forgot to tell you that I talked to the press this afternoon. I had the Captain set it up when I met with him this morning."

"Great. So they're not hanging out at your condo anymore?"

"I hope not. I won't know for sure until I go back there."

"Just not right away, okay?"

His face turned serious. "I want to talk to Emma again. So, yeah, I do want to stay."

"I'm glad you agree."

"I'd like to try in the morning. I'm going to ask for her help."

"And if she doesn't come in the morning?"

"Then I'll have to stay another night."

"Are you moving in?"

It was his turn to laugh. "We should at least have a first date first."

I grinned, and noted that his flirting didn't scare me in the least.

WHEN THE DOORBELL RANG, I opened the door to find the Harmons and Marilee standing on the porch. Nick held a large bundle, and I stepped aside for them to enter. Nick asked "kitchen?" and I nodded in that direction.

Rob shook hands with the Harmons. He bent to Marilee's level and said, "It's great to see you, Marilee," and squeezed her shoulder.

"We wanted to do something to thank you for, you know, for everything," Jane said. "I thought maybe you wouldn't feel like cooking, so we brought over a ham, and the side dishes."

"It smells great," I said. "But you didn't have to do that."

"We wanted to. We owe you so much. Marilee is getting better every day, aren't you, sweetie?" Jane directed a comforting smile at her daughter.

"She's still weak, and she lost a lot of weight, but she's bounced back really well," Jane paused. "Except for the nightmares."

"I'm sorry to hear that," I said, "but not surprised. How could she not have lingering emotional problems after what she's been through."

"Has she talked much about what happened to her?" Rob asked.

"No. She doesn't want to talk about it. Hopefully, a therapist will help her find a way to deal with the trauma she experienced," Jane said.

Marilee's head was bowed and she scuffed one shoe back and forth on the floor.

I looked at her, and my heart almost broke. How could she bounce back from the darkness she'd endured.

TJ came tromping down the stairs at the sound of voices.

I put my arm around his shoulders as he popped up at my side. "TJ, I'd like you to meet Mr. and Mrs. Harmon and their daughter, Marilee."

His eyes widened. "Oh, Marilee! We told Emma you're safe."

"Thank you," she said shyly. "She must be so lonely."

"Who's Emma," Jane asked. "Marilee mentioned her in the hospital."

"She's our ghost," TJ said, a big smile on his face.

"Your what?" Jane responded, turning to look questioningly at me.

"TJ, maybe—" I started to interrupt but he was already launching into a glowing account of our conversations with Emma.

"Maybe you'd better sit down," I said, pulling out a kitchen chair for her. "Nick, you, too."

I turned to TJ. "Honey, why don't you and Marilee go watch TV for a while? The grownups need to talk."

"Okay, Mom." He took Marilee's hand and they disappeared into the front room.

Rob and I took the other two kitchen chairs. I started to offer coffee, but from the strained looks I saw around the table, I sat down again.

"What's he talking about?" Jane asked.

"Kids have such active imaginations," I said, knowing even as I said it that it was an inadequate response, but hesitant to step into what I was sure would be a difficult discussion.

"It doesn't sound like imaginations—" Jane started, but stopped, confusion and concern reflected on her face. "How would your son know about Emma when he's never met Marilee?"

Rob sighed deeply. "Not directly, no."

"And who, exactly, is Emma?" Nick asked.

"Look," I said. "We really don't want to get into this. Marilee's safe now and you should concentrate on helping her get over everything that happened."

"Of course we'll do everything in our power to help her," Jane said. "But she keeps mentioning someone named Emma. If you know who that is, you need to tell us."

"But—" I started, but trailed off. They deserved an explanation, even if it wouldn't make any sense to them. And even if it expanded the possibility the story could get out to the public, which could affect Rob's job.

Rob stared at the table, and lifted his head. "Emma Corning was a little girl who went missing under conditions similar to Marilee's. Eight years ago. She was never found."

"What does she have to do with Marilee?" Jane asked.

"Emma," I started. "Emma's ghost... she led us to Marilee." I held up my hand. "Look, before you say that's impossible, why don't you ask Marilee about Emma?"

"My daughter has been through enough," Jane said with a huff.

"Yes. She has." I had no idea how to proceed. None of us spoke for several moments.

The two kids appeared in the kitchen doorway. Marilee ran up to her mother, her eyes shining. "Mommy! TJ's Dot talks to Emma. Can we get a Dot so I can talk to Emma, too?"

"What's a Dot and what is going on here?" Nick asked, his reddening face reflecting his consternation.

I stood up. "Look. I would have preferred we not get into this, and we wouldn't have if Marilee hadn't brought it up but, since it's the elephant in the room, I'll tell you. You're not going to believe me, and I'm sorry about that, but it is what it is. The Dot is a smaller version of Alexa. You know what Alexa is, right? TJ told me the Dot in his room was crying. I didn't believe him at first, but after a few days I heard the crying for myself. Then a child's voice started asking for help. I was freaked out and we even spent a night in a hotel when it all started but, when I got brave enough, I asked the voice questions, like what her name was. She said her name was Emma. One of the questions I asked was whether she was alone. She said that Marilee was there, too. At that point, I contacted Detective Porter, who was *also* skeptical, until he heard her for himself."

"What she's telling you is the truth, as far-fetched as it sounds. I didn't want to believe the wild story, until I came here and heard it for myself. It was Emma speaking, asking for help. And eventually it was Emma telling us how to find Marilee."

"She did, Mommy. Emma talked to me while I was in that box. She told me not to be afraid, that she was there. I miss her so much."

"Did you see her?" Jane asked.

"No. She just talked to me. I only heard her voice. I wish I could see her."

Jane looked at her, weighing the words, then lowered her head into one hand, rubbing her forehead. When she dropped her hand back into her lap, she looked weary.

"Look," I said again. "I don't know how any of this is possible. I wouldn't have believed it if I hadn't experienced it myself. And Rob's a policeman. Do you think he would blithely accept a story about a ghost?"

"I don't know what I think," Jane said. "But whether it really happened or it was just my daughter's imagination, I'm glad she didn't feel alone."

"Did you find Emma's, uh, remains?" Nick asked.

"No. Not yet. Emma told us Brindleson dumped her in the lake. But it's a big lake."

"So, there's no proof that—"

"No proof yet, but we owe Emma and I'll do everything I can to find her body so that she can move on. The way she's supposed to. We'll be searching the lake in a couple of days. And I'm going to ask Emma for help. If we do find her, you'll have your proof."

Nick tapped his fingers on the table. "I'm sorry, but this seems preposterous." He glanced at his wife, who was watching her daughter. "But I know that you and Kelly saved my daughter, and I'm eternally grateful to you both. So, whatever happened here, we'll leave it be. Is that okay with you, Jane?"

She nodded.

"You can't tell anyone about this," I said. "Please."

Nick looked at me questioningly.

"She's right," Rob said. "Despite your skepticism, it's important you don't repeat what we've told you. Most people would react like you did. Not to mention that it might give Brindleson's counsel a solid argument to have his case dismissed."

"And it could have negative implications for Rob's job," I said. "But it's not just for our benefit. Think about what would happen if the media found out. They're already focused on Marilee. It would be a whole media circus if they heard about Emma. And not in a good way."

"Our lips are sealed," Jane said, her eyes solemn. "You don't have to worry about us. We'll talk to Marilee, too. In the meantime, you should probably refrigerate that ham."

"Eek. I forgot all about it," I said, laughing.

CHAPTER 34

Once I got TJ off to camp the next morning, Rob and I headed for TJ's room. Both of us were nervous, knowing how important it was, fearing Emma wouldn't appear.

"Emma," I started. "Are you here? Can you come out?"

"I need to talk to you, Emma," Rob added. "It's important."

The room stayed warm. We waited, calling out to her several times, but with no success. Rob looked worried, and stood. "Emma. We need you. Now."

I put my hand on his arm. "I'm not sure she'll respond to your angry voice."

He sat down again. "I know. It's just that it's frustrating. I need her help."

"Should we go and try again later?" I asked.

"What's the point? I guess her business with us is done. She was just trying to save Marilee." He stood and walked to the doorway.

"Wait," I said. "I have an idea. I don't know if it will

work, but it's all we've got." I brushed past him as I headed for my room, and was back moments later, dangling my necklace from my fingers.

I clutched it tightly. "Emma, now will you come?"

We only waited a moment before a chill settled over us.

"Emma?" Rob said.

I'm here, she responded. She sounded sad. I'm sure she was lonely.

"I'm coming to find you, Emma," Rob said.

You can't. I'm in the water.

"We have a search team set up for tomorrow, but it's a big lake. Is there any way you can give me a sign to let me know where to look? Anything? If you do, I can dive down there and, with luck, I'll be able to find you."

I'll try, she said. I might have detected a note of hope in her disembodied voice.

"Tomorrow, Emma. Look for me on the lake tomorrow. We'll start from the cabin so you'll know which boat, and I'll be searching the water, waiting for a sign. Okay?"

Okay.

And she was gone.

We looked at each other, and he squeezed my hand and pulled me to my feet.

"Now we wait for tomorrow," he said.

At least there's a chance. We have a chance.

CHAPTER 35

I rode shotgun in Rob's truck on the two-and-a-half-hour drive to the lake. We didn't talk on the way, each lost in our own thoughts. I couldn't go out on the boat with him; it was police business, after all. But I could watch from the dock.

The first boat set out, straight ahead from the dock, then to the left. Rob's boat planned to launch half an hour after the first. He kept scanning the horizon, looking for Emma's sign, seemingly without success. As his boat set out, he looked at me and shrugged, then turned back to scanning the lake.

Biting my fingernails did little to distract me from the stress of worrying. The first boat returned to the dock after an hour, with nothing to report. I watched Rob's boat from the cabin porch as it motored along the shore, then farther out. And I watched when the boat turned back toward the dock. Even from a distance, I could see the defeated look on Rob's face.

He turned slightly to look back over his shoulder, and

did a double-take. Following where I thought he was focused, I saw a waterspout twenty yards behind the boat. Rob pointed and yelled for his crew to turn the boat around. The waterspout stayed in one spot, the water rising fifty feet in the air. Rob sat on the side of the boat as it approached the waterspout, then slipped over the side and disappeared into the lake.

I watched the surface, my heart in my throat, for what seemed an eternity. Divers from the first boat watched from the dock, some pacing as the minutes stretched out. I closed my eyes and prayed.

A cheer erupted when Rob emerged from the water and swam toward the boat. When he reached it, I watched him hand something to one of the crew as he was hauled aboard.

I wanted to run down onto the dock to meet the boat, but wasn't sure of the protocol in a police investigation. And, I didn't want to make a scene in front of his team. They had no idea why we knew the lake had to be searched.

He somehow managed to attach a buoy to the location where he'd made the discovery, of what I didn't know. But it meant something or he wouldn't have needed to mark the scene.

I sank down onto the cabin's porch as I waited for the boat to dock. Then I waited as the divers exited the boat, and as Rob was surrounded, everyone shouting questions. I saw him glance in my direction. Our eyes met and held for just a moment . . . and he smiled.

He started up the path to the cabin as the boat with other divers headed back out on the lake to finish what he'd begun.

"Kelly, I think I found her" he said as he sat beside me on the porch. "God, I'm tired."

"I bet you are. You were down there a long time."

"Only as long as it took," he said with a smile.

"I'd hug you, but you're all wet," I said.

"I'm sorry," he said, hanging his head.

"Heroes don't have to be sorry."

CHAPTER 36

Crap. A missed call from Jeff Silver, the attorney handling the lawsuit contesting Kate's will. I leaned against the kitchen counter, frowning, waiting for the coffee to brew. My frown turned into a smile as I listened to the voicemail. The judge had ruled in my favor. I won.

One less stress I had to deal with. I confess that one had been pushed way into the background by all the Marilee and Emma drama. I'd almost forgotten about it. Still, what a relief.

I carried the coffee mugs out to the living room and handed one to Rob, who was still floating on euphoria from this afternoon.

"Okay. Tell me everything," I said.

"I told you at the cabin."

"I know, but I want to hear it again, in case you forgot anything." Really, I just wanted to listen to him talk.

"Well, to begin with, did you see that waterspout?"

"Did I? Oh my God! It was amazing."

"It was doubly amazing because Emma caused it."

"Did the guys give you a hard time when you said you wanted to dive there?"

"Oh, yeah. It didn't make sense, but I told them I had a feeling and to humor me. I said maybe it was a sign from God."

"I bet that went over well."

"Actually, it did. Anyway, I dropped into the water, and . . . did I tell you how dark it is down there? Visibility wasn't good, and I think the lake might be a hundred feet deep around that area. I have to admit feeling that it would be a longshot to find her, even if she did show me the spot. My flashlight picked up a stream of bubbles maybe thirty feet down and I didn't think twice. I just beelined for that spot. I saw an outcropping where the bubbles were originating. At first, nothing stood out, but I brushed at silt covering a pile of what seemed to be rocks and, when I uncovered them, it was obvious they weren't rocks. Long strands of hair floated in the water and the tiny skull was silently, sightlessly looking at me. There was no doubt it was Emma. I took a bunch of pictures and carried the camera up to the boat. Anyway, that's about the whole story. They should have been able to retrieve the bones by the end of today. They'll let me know."

"And they'll do DNA testing to make sure it's Emma?"

"Yep. I already made the case that another little girl had vanished a few years back and it might be her, so they'll be able to compare the samples."

"Why don't you let me look at your side?" I said. He'd changed out of his wetsuit and back into jeans and a T-shirt at the cabin, so I hadn't been thinking about his wound.

"You don't have to do that," he said.

"I know, but I'm worried what the strenuous activity and being in the water might have done to it. Come on."

I headed for the bathroom and he reluctantly followed.

I noticed him grimacing when he moved to pull the T-shirt off over his head, so I helped him take it off. The wound was still covered by a bandage, but blooms of blood had soaked through. The waterproof bandage had prevented water from getting inside, for which I was relieved.

When I'd adjusted to the sight of the blood, I noticed that Rob was sitting in front of me half naked. I couldn't help myself. I blushed and turned away, busying myself with finding tape and bandages under the sink, so he wouldn't see that I was embarrassed. Being the mother of an 8-year-old, I was pretty well-stocked for any emergency.

"I'm going to change that." When he didn't protest, I started carefully peeling away the bandage. He sucked in a breath and put his hands on my shoulders for a moment.

He looked at me as if he'd done something wrong and pulled his hands back.

"It's okay," I said. "If that helps with the pain, I don't mind."

I carefully washed away the blood and inspected the area around the bullet hole. Thankfully, it didn't look infected, so

I applied some betadine and a new bandage. When he winced trying to stand, I gave him my hand to help him up.

There was a knock at my door. "Are you okay to put your T-shirt back on?" I asked. When he nodded, I went to see who was knocking.

A vaguely familiar woman glared at me when I opened the door.

"Can I help you?" I asked, wondering who she was until it clicked. Tara Edley.

"Tara?" I said, confused and not really confused.

"It's not right that you have this house," she snarled. "You weren't even related to Kate. With your husband dead, you have no connection to this family at all. This house should rightfully be mine."

"I think the judge disagreed with you," I said.

"I don't care what the judge said. The only right thing for you to do is sign this house over to me."

She was making me mad. "And why would I do that? It's my home now. It's my son's home."

"Because. You don't belong here."

"No. *You* don't belong here. You want to know why Kate left the house to Tom? Because he spent his childhood summers with her. His parents rented a house in town and Kate and Tom were best of friends when he was young. I don't remember him mentioning that you were there. Were you? After Tom and I were married, admittedly we didn't see her much, but Tom called her monthly and always remembered her on her birthday and at the holidays. Did you? I don't really know a lot about your branch of the family, but I think, if you'd been as close to her as Tom was, then I expect she would have left you a bigger inheritance."

She sputtered. "How dare you—"

"How dare *me*? How dare *you* come to *my* home like this. Take your greedy ass out of my house and out of my sight. And don't ever come back here again."

She was speechless, her mouth hanging open. If she thought I'd be a meek little mouse and let her bully me out of my home, she definitely didn't know me very well. Or at all.

I slammed the door in her face and glared at it.

"Bravo!"

I turned around to see Rob clapping. "Impressive. Remind me never to get on your bad side."

I felt my cheeks redden. "I didn't tell you I was being sued, did I? She wanted my house."

"So I heard."

"One of Tom's cousins thought I didn't deserve the house because I'm not a *real* relative. I could be sympathetic to that if she wasn't such a butt about it."

"You handled it beautifully. Hopefully, that's the last contact you'll have with her."

He picked up his mug. "Hey, don't you have to go get TJ?"

"Nope. Jen's picking him up. She's dying to come hear

what happened today. I guess you're going to have to tell that tale *again*."

"Maybe I should just write a book."

"You could but, again, you'd probably have to market it as fiction."

He laughed. "Yeah. I guess I would."

"Do you think Emma's gone now? You know, crossed over?"

"I don't know how those things work. My first ghost, after all. According to ghost stories I've read, they leave after their funeral."

"I hope that's true. I want to say goodbye."

TJ AND JEN WERE ENTHRALLED AT Rob's recounting of the events of the day. I'd thrown together a pasta dinner for the four of us because everyone wanted to talk about the unbelievable experiences we'd all shared. After dinner, while the grownups talked, TJ camped out in his room, hoping Emma would drop in.

At the same time, Jen and I noticed Rob's heroic efforts to keep his eyes open, and we took pity on him. She said she needed to get home, and gave Rob a peck on the cheek. "I'll probably talk to you guys tomorrow."

Once he heard the front door close, Rob sat up and stretched.

"Going somewhere?" I asked.

"Yeah, home."

"No, you're not. Stay here tonight. You're exhausted and in pain."

"The neighbors will talk," he said with a tired smile.

"Let them," I said. "You deserve to be pampered."

"I wish I wasn't too wiped out to enjoy it."

"Move over to the chair and I'll get the couch ready. You need to sleep."

The moment his head hit the pillow, he was out. I bent and pulled the blanket up to his shoulders, then impulsively kissed him lightly on the mouth. I surprised myself, and quickly backed away, relieved that he didn't wake up. I rested a hand on his chest, feeling him breathe in and out peacefully. I knew I should go upstairs, but it was hard to leave him.

Maybe it isn't too soon, I told myself.

I walked up the stairs, sticking my head into TJ's room. He looked dejected.

"No Emma?" I asked.

"No."

"I'm sorry. Maybe we'll hear from her tomorrow."

"I hope so," he said.

"Me, too. I'm going to bed. It's been a long day. You should get ready for bed, too. Don't go downstairs. Rob's sound asleep, and he needs it."

"Okay, Mom."

I made quick work of my bedtime rituals, brushing my

teeth and washing my face like I had a time limit, laughing at the thought of falling asleep at the sink. But when I climbed in bed and snuggled under the covers, sleep wouldn't come. Thoughts of Rob swirled through my head. Thoughts of all the times we'd been together, the way he touched me sometimes, always respectfully, his kindness and caring, his growing bond with TJ. The way he felt as close to Emma as I did. The way I didn't want to leave him tonight.

What about Tom? Was I being disloyal by feeling an attraction to Rob? Of course I missed Tom, but missing him wouldn't bring him back. Still, my brain kept screaming Tom! Tom! Tom!

Under normal circumstances, I'd go downstairs and make myself a cup of tea to settle my nerves, but Rob was down there, and I didn't trust myself. When had everything shifted?

I GOT UP EARLY AFTER A FITFUL night and brushed my teeth, pulling my hair up into my go-to messy bun and washing my face. In the light of day, I could face down my attraction to Rob. As quietly as possible, I tiptoed into TJ's room to check on him. He slept peacefully, an angelic smile on his face.

I patted a little foot through the blanket and turned to leave, shivering at the coolness of the room.

He's a good man, Kelly.

My head whipped toward Alexa, my breath caught in my throat, as a chill settled over the room. "Tom?" I managed to choke out.

Don't be afraid to trust your heart.

"Tom!" I wrapped my hands around the Dot, tears streaming down my face. "Tom, wait!" I begged as the room warmed up again.

"Mom?"

I turned to see TJ sitting up in bed, rubbing his eyes. Quickly swiping at my tears, I said, "Good morning, Sunshine. I was just checking on you. Didn't mean to wake you up."

"Will Emma come today?"

"I don't know, honey. I hope so. Are you hungry?"

"Kinda."

"Well, get yourself cleaned up and come on downstairs. I'll get breakfast going."

I don't know how I managed to have that mundane conversation with my son. It felt like a soupy fog had settled over me, and I moved like a zombie down the stairs and into the kitchen, not even glancing in Rob's direction. Had I really heard it? Had Tom told me he was okay about me and Rob? I couldn't help the tears that started to fall again, and grabbed a napkin to dry my eyes before anyone could see.

The kitchen routine helped me control the confusion that wanted to send me back to my room where I could shut out the world.

I heard a sleepy "Good morning," and looked over my shoulder to see Rob leaning against the doorjamb. Rob, with his hair poking up in all directions, wearing a T-shirt and pajama bottoms, his arms crossed, looking like every woman's dream.

Somehow, I managed to smile a normal smile. "I'm just getting the coffee on. Eggs and bacon okay for breakfast?"

"Better than okay. I'm famished."

"You sound like TJ," I said with a chuckle. "Everything should be ready in fifteen minutes if you want to go get ready."

"Thanks, Kel."

No. Thank you, I whispered under my breath. *For healing my heart.*

I felt a peace that had eluded me since Tom's death. I could look toward the future without a shroud of sadness following me into every day.

ROB CALLED FROM THE PRECINCT later in the day to say the DNA match was positive for Emma. It was just a formality, as Rob and I both knew it would be.

"How long before they can bury her?" I asked.

"I'm not sure. Probably two weeks at the outside. They have to examine the body for cause of death. The parents were notified an hour ago. Very emotional, as I'm sure you can imagine. I think they've waited long enough for their daughter."

"I feel so badly for them. I know they probably expected it, but now the fact their daughter is dead is staring them in the face."

"Yeah, I know. I think determining the cause of death will be difficult. If she either starved to death or drowned, they won't be able to tell that from the skeleton."

"Brindleson might get away with it?"

"I don't think so. I'm pretty sure when they analyze materials they found in those enclosures they'll find Emma's DNA there, as well as Marilee's."

"What's Brindleson been saying?"

"He's saying we didn't have a warrant and entered his property illegally."

"Captain Magnusson grilled me on what we were doing there, and I repeated the story about trying to find you lakefront property. He'll back me up, I think."

"Surely Brindleson can't explain away putting Marilee in the boat, can he?"

"A good lawyer will try, but I think the evidence will be enough to ensure that he's found guilty."

"Well, I'm worried."

"Look, nothing is ever for sure. We have to trust that justice will be done here. By the way, Emma's parents are coming to the station tomorrow. They want to thank the dive teams. Do you want to be there?"

"No. They won't have any idea who I am or what my connection might be, and I'm fine with that. You're the one who found Emma, so let them thank you. That's the way it should be."

"I don't think I can get out of it anyway. It's good PR for the department."

"Are you ... are you coming back tonight?" I held my breath waiting for his answer.

"I, uh, I think I've taken advantage of your hospitality for too long. I should go home."

"Oh." I tried to mask the disappointment in my voice, but don't know if I was successful.

"Unless—"

"It's no trouble. Really. I mean, I'm fine if you want to stay another couple of days. You're still in pain and—"

"Are you sure you don't mind?" He gave a half-hearted laugh. "I mean, who wants to say no to being pampered, right?"

"It's settled then. We can try to talk to Emma again."

"I'd like that," he said. I could hear the smile in his voice.

"Dinner's at six. Nothing special, just chicken. I thought it was time for a change from pizza and pasta."

"Sounds great. Not that I don't like pizza and pasta. I can't wait to see you." He sputtered. "I mean—"

"It's okay. I can't wait to see you either." I hung up, wondering if I'd just opened the door all the way. Maybe not all the way, but the door was definitely swinging inward.

Suddenly getting cold feet, I texted Jen to ask if she and Jason wanted to come for dinner. There's safety in numbers.

I added champagne to my shopping list. If the events of the past few days didn't warrant a celebration, nothing did.

CHAPTER 37

"Is someone going to show us this ghost?" Jason asked. "I feel left out."

"Dinner first or ghost first?" I asked with a grin.

"Why wait?" Jason answered.

"Let's go." I had baked chicken in the oven, and the timer wasn't set to go off for another half hour.

On the way up to TJ's room, I tried to tamp down expectations. "She doesn't always come," I said. "She may be spooked by so many people at one time."

"Spooked, huh?" Jason said.

"I know," I said with a laugh. "I just mean I don't know how she'll feel about it. I think everyone should be as quiet as possible and let Rob and me try to contact her."

TJ and I sat on the end of his bed. Rob stood next to me and Jen sat in the rocker, glancing nervously at Jason, who leaned against the doorjamb.

The room temperature was comfortable so it was obvious she wasn't here. I would be disappointed if I didn't get a chance to talk to her one last time. She meant so much to me.

"Emma?" I said. "Are you here?"

Nothing stirred in the room. I looked up at Rob. "You try."

He nodded. "It's me, Emma. Rob. We really want to talk to you. There's so much to say. Please come."

Jen's eyes were big, excited to see what would happen. Jason watched, his face reflecting his skepticism. I wasn't sure what he thought. I was sure he didn't think any of us were lying, and he'd heard the news about the police finding the remains of a little girl named Emma, but I knew it was a lot to swallow without proof.

And, still, Emma didn't come.

As my ace in the hole, I held out my pendant, squeezing my hand around it, closing my eyes and silently willing her to appear.

When the room became suddenly cold and a breeze swirled through the room, Jason's eyes grew huge and his mouth fell open.

"Emma?" I said.

Yes.

"Thank God, Emma. I was afraid you would be gone. Do you know what's happened?"

He found me, she said, and the breeze ruffled Rob's hair. He reached up and touched his face in awe as if he'd felt her hand there.

"Emma, I couldn't have found you without your help. You saved yourself. You're a brave girl. I'm so proud of you."

An eerie giggle came from Alexa. I'd never heard joy from her, and the sound pierced my heart. "Oh, Emma, we love you so much. Can you rest in peace now?"

I can't go yet.

"Did we miss something?" Rob asked, a look of concern on his face.

I want to see my mommy and my daddy.

"There's going to be a funeral for you very soon. Is that when you'll go up to heaven?" I asked.

Yes. It will be finished.

"I'll bury your necklace with you. That's where it belongs."

No. I want you to have it. So you'll remember me.

"Emma, none of us will ever forget you. You're in all our hearts."

"We want you to know, Emma," Rob said. "that we'll all be there for your funeral. To say goodbye."

Can you tell my mommy I want my teddy bear Brownie?

"Of course, I'll tell her," I said, and started to cry. TJ put his arms around me.

"I'll remember you, too, Emma," he said. "You're my friend."

You're my friend, too. Thank you for hearing me. As the chill started to dissipate, a tiny voice said *I love you.*

The room was warm again, and we knew Emma had left the building.

Rob sat beside me and took my hand. None of us spoke

for a moment, then I heard, "What the hell *was* that?" and laughed when I saw Jason's face.

"Told you it was real," Jen said, giving him a hug. "Now you can never doubt me again."

The timer dinged downstairs signaling the chicken was ready. I jumped up and rushed down to the kitchen, everyone following behind me.

When dinner was finished and the dishes tucked away in the dishwasher, I brought out the champagne and poured everyone a glass. I'd bought a small bottle of sparkling apple juice for TJ.

Standing and holding my glass aloft, I said, "We have so many things to celebrate tonight, I don't know where to begin. Our first toast should be to Emma, our brave little ghost. She's the true hero of this story." Glasses clinked around the table.

"I want to drink to Marilee and the miraculous way she's recovered after her horrendous experience." We all took another drink. TJ was beaming as he got to clink his glass to mine.

"This toast is to Rob. For saving Marilee *and* Emma. My heart is fairly bursting with pride for him."

He cleared his throat and wiped at his eyes as surreptitiously as he could.

"Here's to Brindleson being arrested. He can never harm another child." After we all took a drink, I said, "Well, that's about all I can think of."

Everyone set their glasses down and applauded.

Rob stood and raised his glass then. "We need to drink to Kelly and TJ, who listened to a ghost and set the ball rolling so that we were successful in the end. Also heroes."

His eyes met mine. I found myself unable to look away as I felt a warm flush of embarrassment. I hoped no one noticed my discomfort.

TJ wanted to make a toast, and all our attention turned his way. "I want to drink to my mom. 'Cause I love her so much."

"Aww, I love you, too, honey." I teared up as I clinked my glass with his.

JASON AND JEN SAID GOODNIGHT, Jason shaking his head and muttering "I can't believe it," as they walked out the door.

I sent TJ up to get ready for bed and began clearing the champagne flutes off the table. I heard Rob come into the kitchen as I was hand washing them in the sink.

"Can I help you with anything?" he asked.

I felt that warm flush again and shook my head no, not wanting to look at him. When I got myself back under control, I turned around to find him watching me intently. I wanted to touch him, but instead asked if he'd like coffee.

He dropped his gaze, releasing me from the compelling urge to do something I shouldn't do.

"Sure, if you do."

"I'll put some on. It'll only take a few minutes." We sat at the kitchen table then, an uncomfortable silence between us.

Once we had our mugs of coffee in front of us, though, we both relaxed.

"Are you worried about talking to Emma's parents?" I asked him.

"Not really, although I'm in a quandary about what I'll tell them."

"Something occurred to me." I sipped my coffee, looking up at him over the edge of the cup. "This just got complicated. How are you going to ask Emma's parents to bury Brownie with her?"

He looked like I'd punched him. "I hadn't thought about that. I don't have any idea how to tell them."

I watched him silently for a few moments, contemplating the dilemma. When the answer hit me, I jumped up. "I'll be right back."

I tiptoed into TJ's room and took the nanny cam off the shelf and hurried back to the kitchen.

Holding it out to Rob, I said, "If we got any of it on tape, we can show them."

He set the teddy bear on the table. "You're a genius! Whatever the cam saw is recorded on our phones." He started scrolling, with me looking over his shoulder.

I felt chilled when I heard the words "*Can you tell my mommy I want my teddy bear Brownie?*"

He glanced up at me. "This will help. But—"

"What's wrong?" I asked, noticing his scowl.

"How much should we show them? Everything their daughter said? Wouldn't that be horrifying for them?"

"It would be. I don't what them to have to go through that."

"What about just today, when we said goodbye to her?" he asked.

Relief coursed through me. "Of course. We can say that's all we have."

"Then you should come with me when I meet them. You're on that video talking to Emma, too."

"You're right. I'm not looking forward to it, but I'll go with you."

"After our meeting, I'll ask them if they have a moment to talk to someone else who was instrumental in locating their daughter. We don't want to bring the ghost angle up at the precinct."

"The park across from the police station. I could wait for you there."

"That would work. Thanks."

"You don't need to thank me. I want to help any way I can."

He drained his coffee. "Shall we?"

I carried both our mugs to the sink and rinsed them out. "Give me a minute to make up the couch." I paused. "Tomorrow should be interesting."

"I can't imagine how they'll react to hearing the ghost of their daughter speaking."

"I can't either. But hearing that she wants to see them again might bring them some peace. And knowing her spirit still exists . . . won't they find comfort in that?" I said.

"I hope so. I guess we'll find out tomorrow."

CHAPTER 38

I pulled into the parking lot at Piedmont Park. Rob had said to be there around two, and I was fifteen minutes early, so I sat in my car and re-watched the nanny cam video, positioning it to the last conversation with Emma.

I was nervous at the prospect of confronting Emma's parents with a preposterous claim. If not for the video, there would have been nothing we could say to explain the teddy bear request. I took a swig from the water bottle sitting in the cup holder.

There was a clear view of the police department from my parking spot. I waited until I spotted Rob and the Cornings crossing the street into the park, and I got out of the car and walked to meet them.

Emma's parents looked confused. I didn't know what Rob told them, but probably nothing that made sense to them. He introduced us and pointed toward a picnic table off to the right, no one talking until we were all seated.

Mr. Corning looked between Rob and me, finally saying, "Detective Porter told us that you were helpful in finding

Emma. We're very grateful to you for whatever you did."

"We're happy that we could return her to you. Although I'm sure it wasn't the outcome you hoped for."

"No, it wasn't. But after all these years we didn't *really* expect to find her alive. We tried not to give up hope, but it was hard not to expect the worst." He smiled glumly, looking down at his folded hands. "We're not sure why you wanted to speak with us. We've already talked to the police."

I glanced at Rob. "We have a story to tell you. An unbelievable story. We hope it will bring you some peace."

Mrs. Corning's hand went to her throat. "I don't understand."

I took a deep breath before saying, "Do you still have Emma's bear Brownie?"

"Yes. Of course we—" She looked at me sharply. "Wait. How do you know about Brownie?"

"That's where the unbelievable part comes in," I said. I cleared my throat. "Emma told us."

She clutched her husband's arm. "What are you talking about? How could Emma tell you anything?"

"Mr. and Mrs. Corning. Your daughter has been talking to us. Actually, her spirit has been talking to us," Rob said. Before they could protest, he continued. "I know what you're thinking. That it's impossible." I handed Rob my phone, the video queued up. "Which is why we brought this. Before you watch it, you should know that Emma's come through to us several times in the past few days. She helped us find Marilee Harmon."

I could see anger surfacing on Mr. Corning's face. "You should show them the video, Rob," I said.

"Look, we're grateful to you for finding our daughter . . . our daughter's remains, but I doubt there's anything you could show us to convince us that Emma's ghost talked to you. This is disgraceful. Does your department know about this?" He stood and grabbed his wife's arm. "Let's go."

I put my hand on his arm. "Please. This will only take a minute of your time. If we didn't think it was important, we wouldn't expose ourselves to ridicule. Just, please, let us show you."

He shook off my hand, but sat down again. Glaring at Rob, he took the phone as Rob hit the Play arrow.

He found me.

Mrs. Corning gasped when she heard the eerie voice. As the video continued to play, both Cornings were crying.

When Emma said she wanted to see her mommy and daddy, Mrs. Corning buried her face in her husband's shoulder and he put his arm around her.

The video finished, and Mrs. Corning asked to see it again. Both Cornings sat in silence as they watched.

"Is there more?" she asked, hope swimming in her tears.

Rob and I exchanged glances. Rob cleared his throat. "This was the most important message for you to hear. I can email you the clip, if you'd like."

"Of course we'd like," Mr. Corning said. "But you didn't answer the question."

"Mr. Corning, nothing else matters."

"If you don't want us to see the video, can you at least tell us what else she had to say?"

Rob rubbed his jaw and sighed. "Mostly she asked for help. It took awhile before we were prepared to believe our ears but, when she mentioned Marilee, that changed everything. She told us right off that Marilee was still alive, but that she wasn't. She begged us to hurry, as time was running out for Marilee."

"And did she tell you what happened to her? To Emma, I mean," Mr. Corning said.

Rob looked down, reluctant to answer the question. "She did, but it wouldn't do any good for you to know. It's in the past now and even Emma wouldn't want you to try to imagine how she died. Please don't ask to see any more."

Mr. Corning seemed to consider the information. He opened his mouth to speak, but instead ran his hand through his hair. "All right."

"Thank you. Please, find peace in the knowledge that Emma survived. At least her spirit survived, and she'll be there with you at her funeral. That she wanted to see you again. Feel happy that when you put her bear in the coffin with her, it will be the most loving thing for her to take with her as she moves on."

Mrs. Corning looked at me. "The necklace. It was my mother's. Emma thought it was pretty and begged me to let her wear it, and I often did. She was wearing it when she . . .

when she . . . ." Mrs. Corning looked away.

I put my hand over hers, and she gave me a sad smile.

"I thought you'd like to know about the necklace."

"Thank you for telling me. It's what drew Emma to me. I think God must have had a hand in making sure I found it in that antique store," I said, my fingers closing over the pendant. I prepared to lift it off my neck and return it to her. "Would you like to have it back?"

"Oh, no. Please. Emma wanted you to keep it. And so do I. I'm glad I let her wear it. If she hadn't been wearing it . . . if you hadn't bought it . . . I don't want to think about what might have happened. We may have gone the rest of our lives wondering what happened to our beautiful girl."

"I think things happened the way they were supposed to. We can't let ourselves think about . . . any other outcome."

Rob watched us solemnly, then, his gaze steady, he said, "We have to ask you to please not discuss this except among yourselves. As you can imagine, it wouldn't be well-received by the police department, and it would be a media circus if the press got wind of it. For you, as well as for us."

"I understand," Mr. Corning said.

"You said Emma led you to Marilee?" Mrs. Corning asked.

"Emma first came to us for help for Marilee. It was through Emma's words that we were able to put together the pieces of the puzzle. I can honestly say that Marilee wouldn't be alive today if it wasn't for Emma. Your daughter is a hero."

Rob sent the video link to Mrs. Corning, and she clutched her phone to her chest. "Thank you. You gave us our daughter back."

"Your secret is safe with us," Mr. Corning said. "You have our eternal gratitude."

We watched them walk back toward the precinct parking lot. Rob walked with me to my car. When we reached it, I turned toward him. Without a word, he pulled me into his arms. I wondered if he would kiss me, but instead he grinned a crooked grin and let me go. "We did good," he said.

"Yeah, we make a good team."

"A great team." He looked at me and I looked back defiantly. The connection between us crackled in the air. Until he cleared his throat and backed up a step. "Uh, I should get back. I'll stop over this evening for my stuff."

"But, aren't you—"

"You'd probably like to have your house back. I don't want to be in the way. I'm much better, and I don't have any trouble getting around. You've been great, and I appreciate all you've done for me, but I don't want to take advantage."

I wanted to argue. To be honest, I wanted to plead. But I didn't do either. I just nodded and said, "Okay. See you later."

I sat in my car watching him walk across the grass, cross the street and disappear into the police station. My heart ached with tears wanting to fall, but there wasn't time for tears.

It was almost time to pick TJ up from camp. I headed straight to the church and sat in the car while I waited, gazing out the window at nothing. At least, to me it seemed like nothing. The cloud hanging over my head obscured anything outside the car I might have seen.

Had I misread everything? I thought it was me who didn't want to start anything. Maybe he was simply a nice guy with no ulterior motive. That was fine. I mean, nothing really had changed. Even though I'd let the thought of having Rob in my life slip in, I'd just slip it back out. Boy, was my radar off.

The arrival of TJ's bus pulled me out of my malaise, and I plastered a big smile on my face when he came running up to the car. It wouldn't do to let him know his mother's heart was broken again.

With no energy to do anything about dinner, I suggested pizza to TJ and watched him bounce all the way upstairs to get washed up while I placed the order.

I carried the folded sheets Rob had slept on into the laundry room and set them on top of the washing machine to deal with later. I wouldn't need them down here anymore. I really didn't mean to slam the laundry room door behind me.

When the doorbell rang twenty minutes later, I handed TJ a twenty and sent him to collect the pizza.

"Mom," he called from the doorway.

"What do you need, sweetie?" I responded, coming out of the kitchen.

"Delivery for you!"

"I'm not expecting anything," I said, joining him at the front door.

Sitting on a dolly was the rocking horse, wrapped in cellophane, a huge bow around its neck.

"Can you sign for this?" the delivery guy said, sticking the receipt in front of me.

"Oh, sure," I said, not able to take my eyes off the horse. "Who is this from?"

"Don't ask me, lady. I'm just supposed to deliver it. Check the card."

I stepped aside as he wheeled the parcel inside. I directed him to a spot against one wall, took the twenty back from TJ and handed it to the guy. "Thanks," I said, closing the door behind him.

"Who sent it, Mom?" TJ asked. "It's so cool!"

"I don't know," I said, reaching for the card dangling from the bow.

It had to be yours, the card read. *Otherwise, I might never have met you. Love, Rob.*

Love, Rob. It took my breath away. My heart leapt into my throat and my hand flew to my mouth.

The doorbell sounded again and TJ said, "Should I get it, Mom?"

I waved toward my handbag where it sat on the coffee table. "Can you get another twenty out of my purse? It's probably the pizza guy."

He snagged the twenty and headed for the front door. I couldn't tear my eyes away from the horse.

"It's not the pizza guy," a voice said, and I looked up to see Rob grinning down at me.

"Oh, Rob," I cried, jumping to my feet. I threw my arms around his neck.

"Like it?" he asked, smiling down at me.

"I love it." Before I could stop myself, I said, "And I love you."

His eyes searched my face, and I blushed when his gaze traveled to my mouth. He kissed me, but pulled back and looked at me.

Grabbing his tie, I pulled him close, kissing him with a longing I'd been denying for a long time.

Reluctantly, I broke away and buried my face against his chest, his arms engulfing me. He kissed the top of my head and I felt myself glow all the way from my head to my toes.

He wasn't Tom. No. He was Rob Porter. And maybe that was enough.

Actually, it was everything.

Acknowledgments

I want to thank everyone who helped me along the path to bringing "Under the Willows" to publication. Many huge thanks to my sisters Sheila and Michelle, who read through the manuscript, more than once, offering corrections and suggestions. And encouragement! And my niece Elise is always eager to pitch in with proofreading or helping with plot ideas.

I also have to thank my friend Mike Oldham who gave me a couple of storyline ideas that I actually used.

And, lastly, thanks to my wonderful publishing team, which includes Acorn Publishing, Jessica and Holly, my editor Shelly Stinchcomb, Debbie Kennedy for formatting, and Dane at Ebook Launch for the gorgeous book cover.

I also have to express my gratitude to my family and friends for their enthusiastic support.

CPSIA information can be obtained
at www.ICGtesting.com
Printed in the USA
BVHW031006161021
619053BV00043B/37/J